SERENA WILCOX the pizza loving detective is online at:
http://aol/members/writernbt.html

Visit Natalie Buske Thomas' author web site for previews of Serena Wilcox mysteries and updates on new titles.

Enjoy the collection of links for writers, educators and parents.

Check out the message board for current topics or casual chat.

Send Natalie Buske Thomas e-mail at

WriterNBT@aol.com

This book is a work of fiction. Names, characters, places and incidents are products of the author's imagination. While the author draws upon her own life experiences for inspiration, any direct resemblance to actual events, locales or persons living or dead is purely coincidental.

Copyright © 1999 by Natalie Buske Thomas

Published by
Independent Spirit Publishing
P.O. Box 462
Cannon Falls, MN 55009
e-mail: ISPublish@aol.com

Library of Congress Catalog Number: 99-60133
ISBN: 0-9666919-1-1

The Serena Wilcox Mysteries
Book 2

All rights reserved, including the right to reproduce this book or portions thereof in any form whatsoever.

Cover art by Brent Thomas and Natalie Buske Thomas

Printed in the U.S.A.

Virtual Memories

a Serena Wilcox Mystery

Natalie Buske Thomas

Independent Spirit Publishing

Minnesota

To my husband Brent, who was the inspiration for the character Jack.

1

~~~Elizabeth~~~

Tull-tull clicked the candy. *Tull-tull.* He slurped the candy in one noisy sucking motion. Then back to the *tull-tull, tull-tull.* Stewart Lamont rolled the cherry candy with his tongue, clicking it against his teeth.

"Is it dangerous?" Elizabeth Miller asked. Her voice was soft and tentative. Over the phone she was sometimes mistaken for a child. In person, she was often underestimated. Lamont was underestimating her now.

"Of course not, Ms. Miller. It's all 'virtual', which means that nothing is REALLY happening to you in the physical world." Lamont clicked his candy. *Tull-tull.* His eyes were slick, moist and dark, the pits of a rat. His eyes panned Elizabeth's pale legs.

Elizabeth's face flushed. *Of course I know what 'virtual' means, you moron!* Elizabeth worked on the computer daily. She was more than familiar with computer terminology.

Aloud she said, "I mean, are there any side effects?"

Lamont laughed. "No, no. It's pure entertainment, imagination." He clicked the candy. *Tull-tull.*

Elizabeth studied the contract before her. It was simple enough.

Tull-tull.

She filled out the forms and rummaged through her purse for her elusive checkbook. She fumbled past her keys, a wadded Kleenex and a mess of gritty coins before her hand finally hit the vinyl case of her checkbook.

"Do you have any other questions, Mrs. Miller?" *Tull-tull.*

"No, not really." Elizabeth made out the check to Virtual Memories for $150. It was a little steep for a birthday gift, but it was worth it for something so original. Jack would never guess this in a million years.

When she'd heard about Virtual Memories from a feature spot on the evening news she thought about Jack right away. He loved excitement. Elizabeth grinned, thinking about the anticipated reaction to her gift.

Lamont drummed his fingers on the black laminated countertop. He exhaled a hot cherry breath. Elizabeth struggled not to gag.

"When can he use this?" Elizabeth gently

2

arranged the check and the contract on the countertop in an ordered stack. Her dark brown bangs fell across her eyes. She self-consciously brushed them back with her porcelain hand.

"The gift certificate has no expiration date, but I think he will want to use it right away." Lamont smiled at Elizabeth with his small square teeth. The infernal cherry candy was tucked behind his tongue.

"OK then, thanks." Elizabeth slipped the silver Virtual Memories bag into her purse. She'd wrap the gift certificate inside a large box later, to throw Jack's guesses way off.

Tull-tull.

Elizabeth was more than happy to return to the fresh spring outside air. The heavy scent of blooming shrubs was most welcome. Birds were twittering and a lawn mower droned in the distance. Jack would be so surprised, she thought cheerfully.

2

~~Jack~~

Jack whistled the tune he was playing in his imagination while he tipped his chair back, a chair that was not built to recline. He thought about how Elizabeth never got the knack of whistling. Her whistle sounded more like an asthmatic wheeze. Jack laughed aloud.

"Did I miss something?" asked Michelle. She lifted her eyes from the forms she was filling out in black ink to gaze across the office at Jack.

"I was just thinking about something, didn't realize you were standing there." Jack's voice revealed a twinge of embarrassment. He recovered quickly and flashed a boyish smirk at her.

Michelle studied Jack for a quiet second. Then

she gave him a manila envelope.

"You got it done?" Jack's eyebrows shot up in mock surprise. He took the envelope and tossed it into a bin that hosted a stack of paperwork.

"As always." Michelle wet her lips with her tongue and exhaled a long seductive breath. She let her blond hair dangle over her left eye, an eye that was made unnaturally vibrant blue from cosmetic contact lenses. But Jack was oblivious to her charms.

"Good! That means I can cut out early today. Thanks, Michelle." Jack said as he glided toward the door. He scooped up his appointment book, sunglasses and keys in one fluid motion and was out of the building before Michelle could say goodbye.

The warm fragrant air made his steps buoyant as he made his way across the parking lot. In the comfort of his own car, he reflected upon the afternoon ahead. He felt like a boy cutting school on the first golden afternoon of early spring.

He anticipated Elizabeth's reaction to his unexpected short work day. He hoped she wasn't sick again. Sick, tired, and shrinking back from his touch. Of course Elizabeth was not *intentionally* cold to Jack, but she'd stopped returning his kisses a long time ago. Her passion was replaced with exhaustion.

He didn't know if she knew that it was bothering him. Elizabeth was a very giving person, who winced when others felt hurt. So she probably wasn't aware of the problem. But Jack wasn't the type to ask his wife what she was thinking.

There was no question that Elizabeth adored Jack, that he knew. But he sure missed the days when she was crazy and passionate. Ever since their second daughter was born, embracing Jack felt like another errand that Elizabeth performed. Or at least it felt that way.

There were times when he'd even detected a weary look of dread in her eyes when he reached for her. He understood that she often felt overwhelmed by childcare, and he perceived himself to be a reasonable person, but he couldn't help feeling alone when Elizabeth did not respond to him.

It's not that he regretted starting a family. It's just that he didn't expect it to be so emotionally consuming, and imprisoning! They couldn't just hop in the car and go.

Traveling by car was a nightmare, with the oldest one prone to car sickness and the baby fussing to get out of the carseat. But staying at home wasn't easy either. The house was always a mess, with the baby getting into everything every second. He and Elizabeth couldn't even watch TV without constant interruption.

Life couldn't be spontaneous anymore. A simple trip to the store meant packing a diaper bag and getting the girls dressed, which could be a tedious and stressful undertaking. Often Elizabeth didn't take time out to get herself something to eat before they left, so she'd be short tempered and nauseated until Jack stopped to get her a bite to eat.

Then, when they finally made it to the store, it was a tense flight down the aisles. How much shopping would they do before one of the girls began to whine?

    Jack absently rubbed his forehead, driving with one hand on the wheel. He adored his daughters, with their dimpled cheeks and their fullbodied giggles. And he looked forward to their cheery voices greeting Daddy at the door. It was just that sometimes he wished for a nice evening alone with his wife.

    Jack idly wondered what Elizabeth would do for his birthday. Maybe that's why he was brooding over all of this. The whole birthday thing.

    She used to go all out for his special day. But sometime during the past couple of years she'd lost her enthusiasm for indulging him, and instead spent her energies on the kids' birthdays. Which is how it should be, he told himself.

    Yet he was moody and depressed when his birthdays passed uneventfully. Elizabeth's birthdays were *always* that way, year after year, throughout the entire history of their life together.

    He used to tell himself that he'd be more generous when he "made it" in his career, but meanwhile the birthdays passed with no presents, no surprises.

    Things changed for Jack when Elizabeth withdrew. It finally dawned on him that he'd been a jerk. He didn't like that realization. But he was not afraid to admit when he'd been wrong. He wanted to make her face light up before she gave up on him completely. So he did.

    In the dead of winter he had surprised her with diamond earrings that broke the bank. He gave them to her just out of the blue one night after dinner. Elizabeth cried, her tears salty against his rough cheek, her sobs soft and true.

He loved the idea of sweeping her off her feet. He saw a spark in her that hadn't been there in a long time. He couldn't even remember the last time he'd seen her eyes dance like that. Jack was proud of that moment.

Things had been more lively between them since that day, a few months ago, but Elizabeth was still tired at the end of a long day with the kids. While the diamonds had been a nice first step, Jack had to pay attention to his marriage.

This was a new and unwelcome development from the early days of their marriage in which Elizabeth doted on him. Back then, he did whatever he wanted. He took his wife's passion for granted. It's not that he ever stayed out late. Jack was the type to come home after work. But he didn't feel inspired to go the extra mile, doing the whole romance thing. He felt silly acting like he was dating his wife. They'd been married over ten years.

Jack pulled the car into the driveway. The garage door was open. A pink plastic tricycle with sparkly streamers on the handlebars was lying in the middle of the garage floor. Beside it was a bottle of soap bubbles and a purple dinosaur. Jack sighed.

He got out of the car to move the tricycle, then pulled the car into the garage. As he neared the door to the kitchen he could hear Elizabeth's strained scream at the kids, "*I said, **NO!***"

Swell, he thought. Another day at the Miller house. What was left of Jack's spring fever mood trickled away before he walked in the door. Today was his birthday, the big Three-Oh. Another day in his life, the life of a family man.

Jack hated that he wasn't in his twenties anymore. Twentysomething felt young. He and Elizabeth went to college together and would pull all-nighters, working on a project and eating pizza into the wee hours of the morning. Now pizza gave him heartburn and ten o'clock was bedtime.

Jack remembered when his *own* parents were in their thirties. They seemed old to him then. At the time he never expected to be thirty. But the time had passed so quickly and here he was.

He couldn't imagine how forty would hit him if thirty felt this bad. Then fifty and sixty. Well, it was all downhill from here.

Thirty was young to the old, but old to the young. Jack had never been old to the young before. He hated the feeling. He hated seeing doctors younger than himself, he hated the way bank tellers called him "Sir" and he hated the budding love handles hugging his back.

Jack had worked himself into such a funk, that when Elizabeth finally gave him his birthday gift later that same evening, he had to force himself to show any enthusiasm. It was too little too late. Hadn't she noticed how he was feeling? Where was the big surprise party?

He needed to be babied, he needed to feel that it was an OK tradeoff to be thirty and married with children. He wanted his ego stroked.

Even the gift itself was disappointing. He'd been expecting a new shirt or maybe that flight simulator computer game he had his eye on. But a gift certificate to "Virtual Memories"? *What was she thinking?* She sure wasn't thinking about *him*.

Jack didn't even know what Virtual Memories *was* until Elizabeth explained it to him. He vaguely remembered hearing something about the high tech games on the news and he passed the Virtual Memories brick building nearly every day, but never did he express any interest in checking it out.

After hearing more about it he still had zero interest in Virtual Memories. Jack wasn't a touchy-feely sort. Sentimental memory stuff didn't sound at all appealing to him. Especially commercialized sentiment. He hoped that Elizabeth didn't spend that much on it. He guessed that he'd be better off not knowing how much money she wasted.

He was stuck going, on a Saturday no less. Elizabeth had set the whole day up for him. They'd have dinner together after his Virtual Memories session. With the kids, of course. Elizabeth didn't like to hire a baby-sitter. Even if he *could* talk her into hiring one, she'd be fretting about the kids the entire evening. So what was the point?

That night Jack looked at his wife as she slept. She was quietly snoring, from the far side of the bed.

The baby's tiny body was sprawled out in the middle of the bed, between the two of them.

Elizabeth had fallen asleep while breastfeeding the baby. Her dark hair was spread across the pillow like a silky fan. Jack touched her cheek. Her delicate porcelain skin was as soft as rose petals, as soft as the baby's skin. Both females smelled sweetly of shampoo and sugar cookies.

Jack reached out to touch his wife again. Elizabeth groaned and slid further away from him. Jack groaned, agonized. He lay still, listening to the baby's squeaky snoring.

"Happy Birthday to me...." he whispered sarcastically.

3

~~~Virtual Memories~~~

Jack leaned against the black laminated countertop. Within seconds a man about his own age and height, 6 feet even, greeted him with a healthy warm handshake. The man was a bodybuilder. His muscular frame bulged beneath the snug purple "Virtual Memories" polo. *I'd work out too if I was single*, Jack rationalized, thinking of his own flabby middle.

"Cashing in a gift certificate? Great gift, you'll enjoy it." The man's badge said "Dan the Smilin' Man". Dan had jet black hair that crowned his head in curls. Tall, dark and handsome. With good teeth.

"I'm not sure I even understand what it is that you do." Jack decided to be frank. If he felt too squeamish about this, he'd back out. A gift certificate didn't obligate him to anything. Even though the money came from his own bank account, the one he shared with Elizabeth.

"Well, let me take you into our Virtual Room. I'll cover our standard game package, and answer any questions you might have." Dan grinned a college-boy, football-hero smile. He swung a gold plated key ring around his meaty thumb and lumbered around the counter toward Jack.

"How long does this thing take?" Jack hated feeling hustled by salesmen. He wanted to make it clear that he couldn't be swept away by marketing hype.

"If you'll follow me through this door, I'll discuss the program in our Virtual Guestroom." Dan's broad shoulders brushed past the narrow door frame. Even the back of his neck was muscular.

Jack followed "Smilin' Dan" into an empty room covered in black velvet and washed in purple light. Jack rolled his eyes. *How hokey can you get?*

"Yo, Elvis, you in here?" Jack called. He couldn't imagine what people saw in this stuff. Rich people are weird, he thought.

Dan laughed politely, then shut the door behind them. "All right, Jack, if you'll stand right here, we'll get started." Dan indicated the neon "X" tape mark on the floor.

"What?" Jack coughed mockingly into his fist. "I'm not doing *any*thing until you explain all of this."

"OK." Dan smiled patiently.

"So? What is the deal with this room?" Jack threw up his hands in a sweeping motion.

"This is the equipment we use to simulate the

memory events. You'll be wearing our patented headset and gloves. We've eliminated the need for a body suit." Dan said.

"And what are they for?" Jack stood with his arms across his chest, holding his ground several feet away from the X tape mark on the floor.

"The goggles and gloves allow you to be a part of the memory session. You will be able to feel things, even smell things. It will feel like a live event." Dan said proudly.

"Hmm."

"Are you ready to give it a go?"

Jack shrugged his consent and stood on the X. He was immediately startled by a whirring sound above his head. A headset was lowered by cable to suspend in the space in front of him.

Ooh, snappy special effects for rich freaks, he thought sarcastically.

Dan's voice boomed at him, "Put the headset on, I will make sure it's secured." He remained overly professional, absorbed in thought about the next step on the list.

Jack snorted. But he put the thing on. It was like a diver's mask. He wondered if they ever cleaned it after untold numbers of people before him had worn it.

Dan gave Jack sleek black gloves. He waited for him to put them on. Then he adjusted the gloves at the wrists with velcro tabs.

"You'll be asked to drink the Memory Enhancing Shake at the prompt." Dan said hesitantly.

"The Memory *what*?" Jack grinned.

"Don't worry, the drink is safe in moderation."

Dan said. He noted Jack's skeptical expression, but his own face was unreadable.

"In moderation?" Jack lifted an eyebrow.

"None of the ingredients are controlled substances." Dan said defensively.

Jack laughed. "Then I don't need to worry about the drive home?"

"No worries." Dan smiled.

"OK. So headset, gloves and drink." Jack couldn't wait to find out where all of this was going. He couldn't see Dan very well through the headset, so he was already impatient to get the thing off his head.

"In a few moments you will be walked through our program by our Virtual Guide. After this introduction to the program, what we call our Virtual Tutorial, I will answer any questions you may have." Dan's voice sounded far away to Jack's ears.

Jack heard the door close behind Dan. The thought of being alone in a black velvet room was so ridiculous that he wanted to rip the headset off and go home. But sudden light and sound cut off his impulse to bolt.

He inhaled sharply as the show began.

It was incredible, like watching a movie *inside his head!* The colors, the images, the intensity of the audio... It was *real!* He felt like he was awake while dreaming. Even better than that.

Jack knew he was only watching a computer animation file through rubber goggles, but he had to remind himself of that over and over again. The sensations were so overpowering, so true to life, so *real!* It was absolutely amazing. It was hard to believe it wasn't real. How could he see and feel and even *smell* something that wasn't really *there?*

"Welcome to Virtual Memories," said a masculine voice. A three dimensional logo hovered somewhere in front of Jack. He vaguely recognized the logo as the symbol that was on Dan's polo.

Jack wanted to reach out and touch the logo, to remind himself that there was nothing *really* in front of him. He couldn't get over how real it looked, a computer graphic floating in front of him, alive! He reached his gloved hand out to touch the image, and felt an odd sensation in his hand, as if he'd touched something cool and smooth. No way! *How did they do this?*

"Our basic package is a 30 minute session involving the memory of your choice. Relive the memory, enjoy the experience." The voice materialized into the image of a man who looked like the real life "Smilin' Dan". It was too much, watching a man who had just walked out the door suddenly appear before him, suspended in midair. Dan was so "alive" in the virtual version of him that Jack smelled a trace of his cologne.

Jack watched the "Virtual Dan" use a pointer, indicating the controls on the side of the goggle apparatus that Jack was wearing. There was a volume button and a switch for ejecting the remote control pad. Whoa, too high tech. Jack wasn't into sci-fi stuff. He hoped this thing would end soon.

Virtual Dan flashed a smile, "For your refreshment, and to enhance the chemical activity in your brain, please drink your Memory Enhancing Shake now." He used the pointer again, showing Jack a table he didn't notice before.

There was a child-sized coffee cup on the table. Jack's throat was dry and he was grateful to have the chilled smooth liquid to drink. It was hard to drink the shake with the headset on, but a long flexible straw made it possible. The drink was fantastic, icy with a mild chocolate flavor. Not cocoa or chocolate milk. It was almost a chocolate soda. He didn't give much thought to what the drink was for, figuring it to be a gimmick, the mumbo jumbo about enhancing the chemical activity in the brain.

"Use the remote control to make new selections," Virtual Dan was saying. "Use the up and down arrows to move around in your memory files. Use the numeric keypad to select a starting date from which to search for a memory." It was not unlike the remote control for a TV or VCR.

Jack studied the remote control in his hand. It was a little hard to see the numeric pad through the images displayed in the goggles, but he could make out the glowing numbers. As his eyes adjusted to the darkness the numbers were easier to see.

It felt strange to touch the keypad. His senses were so heightened that the light touch of his skin on the keypad overwhelmed him. His brain was so charged, so alert. He was electric, yet mellow, a sensation that reminded Jack of being in the throes of a dream state: the mind is racing along in a dream while the body is in a deep slumber.

Select a date now, to make a memory selection.

    Virtual Dan smiled and faded from view. Jack realized belately that he'd given no thought to what memory he'd choose.
    All was dark and a bottomless purple in the Virtual Guestroom. Jack looked at the glowing numbers on the remote. Shrugging his shoulders, he keyed in 1987, the year he graduated from high school. He pressed "Enter".
    Virtual Dan returned. A visual of the remote control pad was hovering in front of Jack, so close he could touch it. *If* it were real. Jack wondered what the deal was. He didn't believe that he'd actually see his past looming in front of him, so how long would this game go on?
    Dan used the pointer again, "You have selected a year. If you do not know the specific date you would like to visit, please use the up and down arrows to surf around your memory files. When you find a date you would like to select, hit 'Enter'."
    Virtual Dan faded away. Jack pressed the up arrow key. He didn't know what to expect, but he sure didn't believe that he would see his own memories. He waited in the darkness for a few short seconds.

    The vibrant light was overpowering at first. It took a few seconds for his eyes to adjust to the brightness, but then he could make out shapes.

Within seconds his vision was clear and more sharp than ever before.

It was *his life*. Jack felt the hairs on the back of his neck standing on end. His heart was racing. This couldn't be happening! *How could this be him, his own past? How was it possible?*

"Mom, just a few more minutes!" It was his own voice, and it *felt* like it came from him. But it was the voice of himself at seventeen, a slightly higher pitch than the baritone he had today. He really felt like he was this boy, the young Jack.

He was in his childhood bed in his parents' house. He smelled bacon grease. He heard his sister's voice rise and fall. He felt the heaviness of his grandma's quilt around him. His own blond hair was damp with sleepy sweat. He was *there*.

The scene vanished. Purple darkness descended upon Jack like a fog. A fog of dreams that are forgotten when sleep is interrupted.

"The selection you are viewing is January 1, 1987. Please indicate your interest in this selection by pressing 'Enter'." Virtual Dan had returned.

Jack blinked in the darkness. He swallowed a few times and realized that his throat was dry. He had been home again, really home again. He had long forgotten the brown train wallpaper in his room, his grandma's colorful quilt that had fallen apart in the washer years ago, and the way that a delightful smokey haze from breakfast drifted up to his room.

It was all coming back to him, the peace and comfort of childhood. He didn't want to leave. But he obediently pressed 'Enter'.

Virtual Dan smiled. "Very good. You have

learned how to navigate our basic program. Thank you for joining us here at Virtual Memories."

Click!

The Virtual Dan character was gone. The room was bathed in violet light. Someone was releasing the goggle straps from around his head.

The real life Smilin' Dan sang, "So, what did you think? Impressive, huh?" He shook Jack's shoulder with a playful tug. He waited for Jack's reaction, his smile bright.

"What? That's it? I didn't get to do my selection." Jack felt cut off, deflated. Never before had he felt so connected to himself. He wanted to return there, to that safe place between sleeping and waking. He *needed* to return.

"You can make an appointment to set a date for your first Virtual Memories session. This was a walk-through to teach you how to use our basic program." Dan smiled again, showing a lot of nice looking teeth.

"But why have me drink the shake and all of that, just for a few minutes? I didn't even have time to digest it." Jack said, miffed.

"We like to show you the whole routine, as a trial run. The shake won't hurt you." Dan explained.

"Oh, OK." Jack shrugged. Guess he'd be back, hmm. He wondered if Elizabeth knew that this thing was so involved? Probably not.

Dan continued with his Virtual Memories jargon, "You'll have 30 minutes of uninterrupted Virtual Memory experience when you return for your session." He held the door open for Jack. "Just follow me out this way, and we'll see what date works for you."

4

~~~The Office~~~

Michelle tapped her foot in a crazy nervous rhythm. She studied Jack's face as he murmured into the phone. She knew he was talking to his wife. Elizabeth called the office a couple times a day. Sometimes Michelle could hear what they were saying, especially when she quietly picked up on the other line, as she was doing now.

"Is Tylenol bringing the fever down?" said Jack with a weary note in his voice. He ran his hand through his blond locks, hair that was usually cut too short for his fingers to pass through. He reminded himself to ask Elizabeth to give him a haircut this weekend.

"Seems to be, at least so far." Elizabeth's voice

was barely audible over the steady whine of one of the girls, probably the baby.

Michelle imagined Elizabeth standing in the Miller's kitchen, phone to her ear, with the baby on one hip. She watched Jack from her own desk across the room. He was playing with a pencil, tapping it on his desk. *He's annoyed with her*, Michelle thought.

"That's good. If she gets any worse, let me know." Jack dropped the pencil and tipped back in his chair, balancing it on two legs. He reached for some of the paperwork in his "in" box. He leafed through the papers, probably not really reading the words on the pages.

Michelle leered. Jack's tone was dismissive. *Elizabeth has to notice that*, she thought.

As if she could read Michelle's thoughts, Elizabeth said, "Were you busy when I called?"

"No, why?" Jack said.

Michelle nearly giggled aloud. Jack's voice was flat, rude.

"You acted busy, that's all." Elizabeth glanced down at the baby, who was starting to fuss in earnest.

Michelle thought she detected an anxious lilt to Elizabeth's voice, a whine to match the steady wail of the baby. She imagined Elizabeth frowning in worried concentration. Oh poor, poor Elizabeth, what did you ever *do* to make hubby so frustrated, she thought mockingly.

"I do need to get going." Jack's voice was a few degrees cooler.

There was a momentary silence that was laced with tension. Michelle felt a tickle in her throat and feared that she'd cough. Surely any sound near the receiver would be heard, by Jack especially. He'd hear it in stereo. She felt her stomach wave, not from hunger, although it was nearly the lunch hour, but from nerves.

"OK, well, I better let you go," said Elizabeth. Her voice trailed off, lost inside the turmoil of various unexplained jarring noises invading her kitchen. The baby was still fussing, dishes were clinking and the older daughter was demanding to be fed.

Michelle lifted her eyes over the computer monitor. She could see Jack sitting at his desk. His head was bent, so he wouldn't notice her looking at him. She saw him shrug his shoulders, a typical Jack gesture.

"OK, I'll talk to you later then." Jack started to pull the phone away from his ear, then must have thought better of it, and waited for his wife to speak.

"Love you." Elizabeth's voice was as soft as a kitten's meow and oozing with the same helpless cry. Love me back, it said.

"Love you too." Jack's voice was not so loving. Jack hung up the receiver. He spun swiftly to his feet and was at Michelle's desk in a flash with a surly look on his face. A pink hue to his skin, the vein on his forehead prominent.

Michelle gasped and swallowed air. Caught red handed. The phone dangling in her manicured fingers. Elizabeth had only *just* hung up. Surely Jack knew what she'd been doing.

"Michelle, I'm leaving for lunch, I might be back a little late." Jack didn't even look her in the face before he was out the door. He walked in quick angry strides with his head bent.

She waited for the door to latch behind him before she breathed. She put the phone on it's cradle. That was close, too close. She vowed to be more careful in the future.

5

~~~Dan, The Smilin' Man~~~

Dan entered Jack's customer profile into the computer system. Jack seemed like a sharp guy, he should get a kick out of what they were doing at Virtual. How could he *not* be impressed?

Dan had been working in the entertainment business ever since he dropped out of college over a decade ago. But nothing else compared to Virtual Memories. Virtual was by far the most sophisticated program he'd ever seen.

And talk about a class act, it was definitely created for the bored and the *wealthy*. $150 bucks for a starter session was a teaser. Once players got hooked, they would be shelling out $300 or more each game. There were a number of "Add ons" too, that raised the price into the *thousands* for one game.

And people paid it, gladly. Some customers came as often as once a week. Most of them could easily afford the high tech entertainment, but there were a few customers that really shouldn't be playing. Dan felt a twinge of guilt when this happened.

He often tried to counsel such a client, but it didn't always work. Some of those people seemed almost addicted to the sessions. Sort of like needing therapy maybe. He wasn't sure.

Dan was there when Virtual first opened it's doors six months ago. No one knew then if it would be a hit or a flop. His family raked him over the coals about him starting on yet another new venture, but now even they were impressed. Dan was flashing a hefty wallet around town, making a salary in the triple digits. He had invested some of his own money when he'd been hired on. He had to, all the top management were owners. It smelled of a scam, he knew, but he'd gone with his gut instinct that it was the real thing— a real life get-rich-quick deal. He knew *somebody* always made a lot of money when new markets were discovered, why not him?

Dan wasn't the type to play the lotto. But he did dream of big money, money he wanted to earn the hard way. He was driven by his passion to *be* somebody. With each new turn in his career he plunged himself into his work even more fervently, mind, body and soul.

This time his determination was paying off.

Of course he *could* be working behind the video store counter today, just as easily. He had taken quite a risk in leaving his previous managerial position to take up with a new business. It was good fortune that his hunch about Virtual Memories had been right.

Dan knew he could thank God, and his faith, for the direction his life was taking. He focused on the mini-poster affixed to his computer monitor with blue putty. It said, "Pray as if it's up to God, then work as if it's up to YOU."

Dan loved that motto, even though it sounded like a greeting card verse. He adopted it as his own mantra. Faith and work, work, work. That's how he got where he was today.

And he loved his job. The best part was that he made people's dreams come true. It was heartwarming to see how peaceful even the most troubled clients were after a few Virtual sessions. They visited their most healing memories, often after Dan prodded them in that direction. He considered himself to be an amateur shrink of sorts. A counselor, a friend.

So what if he hadn't become a doctor, a scientist, a teacher, a religious leader, or a politician? As one of the top managers at Virtual Memories, he was often more than that. He helped people heal themselves. He gave them their past.

Which brought his thoughts back to his newest client. Jack Miller. What made him tick? The man with the Nordic blue eyes was an enigma to him.

Jack was intelligent, probably highly intelligent. He seemed to have his act together in a good job. He was supporting a young family. And yet, there was a wistful quality to Jack that raised a red flag.

Dan noticed that Jack had selected the memory file of his senior year in high school. It was a common choice, so maybe it meant nothing. But sometimes it hinted at a man who was unhappy in his adult life. Dan made a mental note to ask more questions. He was good at his job, he could help Jack Miller. Whatever the man was searching for, Dan felt sure that the answers would come from within. If the past would help Jack, Dan was the man to give it to him.

6

~~~Session One~~~

Jack kissed Elizabeth on the cheek. "Bye, honey, see you later!" He headed down the Miller's cracked sidewalk toward the car, then doubled back to the house.

"Forget something?" Elizabeth dangled Jack's car keys out the front door. She laughed, a soft lilting laugh that Jack was fond of. He hadn't heard that laugh in what felt like ages. Maybe Elizabeth was adjusting to life with two small children.

He took the keys, and another kiss. It was worth the surprised, and *pleased*, glimmer in his wife's eyes. "Thanks again for the birthday present," he said gleefully.

Elizabeth sang, "I knew you'd love it!" She

smiled prettily and waved at Jack as he drove away. She stood in the doorway watching him.
"See ya!" Jack called out the window.
"Bye, Daddy!" shouted Kimmie. She twirled her dainty three year old hands in vigorous waving. Her nose pressed against the screen when she yelled. "Bye! Bye!"
"Bye!" Jack matched his daughter's lung power. He waved at Kimmie until he could no longer see her blond head bobbing up over the window sill.

~~~ ~~~

Smilin' Dan greeted Jack with a generous clasp on the back. "Are you ready for your first session, Jack?" Dan was wearing another Virtual Memories polo shirt. This one had vertical stripes which made him look taller.
"Sure I'm ready!" Jack eagerly followed Dan down the long corridor. They passed the black velvet room.
Jack paused in his steps, gesturing toward the door to the room he thought of as The Purple Room. "Why aren't we going in here?"
"I think you'll be more comfortable in our Virtual Suite." Dan opened an oak door and gestured for Jack to go in. He held a smug expression, knowing how pampering the Virtual Suite was. Jack would love it.
"Whoa! Cool." Jack gawked at the plush surroundings; a high-backed leather reclining chair, pillowy and inviting, wall to wall satin pile carpeting,

and track lighting. His dream room. A few minutes in that chair would be worth the bucks.

Near the chair was a glass and marble table. Jack noticed a stone mug, probably filled with that delicious drink he'd had during his first visit. *Ah, it doesn't get any better than this*, he thought.

"Take a seat, Jack. Relax. Listen to music. The remote for the CD player is located under the left armrest. The Virtual Memories selection remote is under the right armrest." Dan showed Jack the collection of CDs, on the shelf under the glass table.

"Take your time. Drink your Memory Enhancing Shake. I'll return in a few minutes to prepare you for your first session." Dan gave a friendly salute and left Jack alone in the suite.

Jack allowed his body to sink slowly into the creamy leather folds of the chair. He exhaled noisily. He remembered the CD remote and began to fiddle with the buttons. *Oh, the drink*, he thought. This was the life.

The shake flowed down his throat, filling his senses with a pleasant awareness of chocolate. Jack let his eye lids close. The lids felt warm and heavy. He let his shoulders relax, then his neck. His breathing became slower and deeper.

"Jack," said a masculine whisper. Dan gently shook Jack's shoulder.

"Huh?" Jack shook the cobwebs out of his head and grinned sluggishly. "Sorry, I must have dozed off. Too comfortable." He glanced around the room, groggily remembering where he was.

"I don't blame you. Two minutes in that chair and I'd be out too." Dan grinned.

Jack suspected the man was just being polite, but he appreciated it anyway. "I think I'm ready to get started. I don't want to doze off again."

"No problem. I'll help you figure out how to secure the headset." Dan unlocked a cabinet and brought out a fur lined contraption. It looked like a hunting hat suitable for the arctic air of northern winters. The plastic goggles were barely detectable.

"I hope you aren't claustrophobic." Dan said with a question in his voice.

Jack laughed, "No, not yet. Maybe I will be after spending time in that thing!"

"It does look intimidating, doesn't it? But you'll forget it's on once you get caught up in the session." Dan assured him.

"Wow, are you sure all of this is included in the gift certificate?" Jack's eyebrows rose.

"Yes, we like our clients to enjoy their sessions. If you like it, you might come back." Dan smiled.

"The gift certificate was offered at an *introductory* price, huh?" Jack finally caught on.

"Sorry, we can't offer you this price the next time around, it's a one-time offer. I'm sure you can see the value of our program for yourself." Dan adjusted the headset straps to fit Jack comfortably.

"It's really incredible, but it's probably out of my league." Jack cracked his knuckles, a nervous habit he had whenever money was discussed.

"Enjoy your gift session. Do you have any questions?" Dan shifted the subject away from the unpleasantness of the session fees and money.

Jack sat up straight, afraid Dan was leaving

the room. "Now what do I do again? I use the remote to choose a date, or pick any year and then use the arrow keys to look around?" Jack held the remote in his right hand.

"Yes, that's it. You'll have 30 minutes. When your session is over, the power will shut off and the lights will come back on automatically." Dan frowned at his watch. He needed to get Jack's session started before it delayed all of the other sessions he had scheduled that day.

"OK, no problem." Jack was eager to get started.

"You should remain seated until I return. Then I will help you remove the headset. Any questions?" Dan waited.

"No," said Jack. "I'm ready."

"OK then, I'll be back after your session is over. Enjoy!" Dan lightly slapped Jack's upper back on his way out of the room.

Click.

The door latched and the lights dimmed. The room was hazy with a violet fog. A mist that seemed warm, humid, and delightful. Like the air after a hot summer's rain.

Whoosh!

The Virtual Memories logo appeared, joined by a soundtrack, then a voice. The lights and sound engaged Jack, making him feel the excitement of a boy on the best rollercoaster in the park.

"Make your selection, please" said the voice.

Oh, that's right, once again I forgot to think this through thought Jack. He held the remote with both hands. What day should he choose?

Jack liked his demo session experience, and couldn't come up with any other ideas. He punched in the year he'd visited before, 1987. He pressed 'Enter'.

It was the same scene he'd experienced before. He was in bed, under his grandmother's quilt. His mother was calling for him. Breakfast was cooking downstairs. He was transported to the past, a past where life felt safe.

Jack wanted to get out of bed and look around his childhood home, to remember it all. But the young Jack went back to sleep. Deep and cozy under the quilt, sleeping like only a teenage boy can.

The real Jack was in a stupor, powerless to do anything. While "Virtual Jack" snoozed, the real Jack could barely move.

Ugh, thought Jack, *I don't want to waste my session sleeping!*

With great effort he managed to grasp the remote. He hit the arrow key a few times, then let go of the button. He'd forwarded the time a few weeks into the future. It was January 1987.

It was early afternoon. He was in school. He could smell the cafeteria food, he could feel the rush of air as students brushed by him in the corridor, he could sense the burden of a stack of books clutched under his left arm.

Virtual Jack stopped at a dented metal locker. He spun the combination lock until it opened. To his amazement, the combination of the lock was sharp in the real Jack's memory, 8R-24L-15R. He exchanged some books. Then he shut the locker door, merging into the crowd again.

He couldn't see much, only kids' bodies moving around him. Occasionally he caught glimpses of the corridor. In a few minutes he was in a classroom. *What an ordeal that was*, he thought. *No wonder I always hated school.*

Virtual Jack sat at a desk. The desk felt cool and moist. It was probably laden with bacteria, thought the real Jack. There was a ventilation fan humming overhead. Mold spores in that, probably. The whole building was dirty and decaying.

Jack's history teacher cleared his throat and then greeted the class, "We'll pick up where we left off yesterday at the end of World War 2..." Chalkdust handprints decorated the man's navy pants. The brown sweater vest he wore was so dated looking to Jack's modern eyes.

For the next several minutes the real Jack studied one of the favorite teachers of his youth. He appreciated the man even more now, as he looked at him through the eyes of an adult, an adult who understood how challenging it is to teach children. How the man had the patience, he didn't know.

He admired the way Mr. Kuhr drew the kids into the discussion. The man was kind to the students, and best of all, interesting. Too bad the young Jack hadn't been more grateful. Virtual Jack was slumped in his chair, barely keeping his eyes open. It was making the real Jack sluggish again. *Wake up and show some respect*, he wanted to tell himself.

Jack clicked on the arrow button to move on to something else. Ah, now it's getting fun, he thought. The Virtual Jack was on a ski club outing. It was the only time in his life that he was a downhill skier. He remembered being quite good, too. He relished the thought of himself as a fit young man, an athletic man.

While the Virtual Jack stood in the frigid air, chatting casually with his friends, the real Jack's body temperature decreased. He felt chilled. His nose was numb, his cheeks were icy to the touch. His toes ached. He longed for the Virtual Jack to go back inside. *Eat some fries in the lodge cafe*, he silently begged himself.

The Virtual Jack was talking to his friends. "Paul, you gotta try the jumps."

"You done those?" said Paul. The real Jack squinted hard at the face before him. He didn't know this kid from Adam.

"Yeah, I did it last time—"

Click.

The lights flicked on. The audio and visual cut off simultaneously. Smilin' Dan was unfastening the headset. It all ended so abruptly that Jack was disoriented.

"How was it, Jack?" Dan asked cheerfully.

"I can't believe how real it felt. It was like going back in time." Jack stood up. He felt groggy, and his head felt like he'd been swimming in chlorine for hours.

"A lot of our clients explain it that way," said Dan. "The lounger is their time capsule."

"Yeah, I can see that. But sort of. It was a total body experience, yet I was aware that I had not really gone anywhere." Jack struggled to explain it.

"I think I know what you mean." Dan guided Jack out the door, anxious to keep the sessions on schedule, yet not wanting to hurry Jack.

"It wasn't what I expected though." Jack said reluctantly. "And it sure was a fast half hour."

"You were disappointed with your session?" Dan's eyebrows furrowed.

"Not with the technology, it's just that it's not as much fun as I thought it would be to be a teenager again. I'll pick something better the next time."

Next time? Dan smiled to himself. Yes, Jack would be back. *Good*, he thought.

7

~~~Wilcox Detective Agency~~~

"I can't believe that you can eat all of that," said Karyn.

"I eat as much as a growing boy, yeah, I know, I hear that a lot." Serena grumbled as she dabbed the corner of her mouth with a brown paper napkin.

"No, I mean I can't believe you can eat all of *that*. It's disgusting! Pools of grease floating on top, really Serena, ICK!" Karyn chuckled. Being with Serena was like being with a childhood girlfriend even though the two had known each other for only a short while.

Karyn met her after she'd hired Serena to look into her husband's strange activities. She learned that the man she was married to wasn't even her lawful husband, a complicated tale that left her delightfully single. A woman with a healthy bank account, Karyn was now working at Wilcox Detective Agency for peanuts, or in this case, pizza.

"You realize that we might not see a case anywhere close to as interesting as the one you hired me for," mumbled Serena behind a mouthful of mozzarella.

"What cases *do* we have?" Karyn averted her gaze from her friend's feast. It was not a sight to behold.

"None so far." Serena said with exaggerated nonchalance.   Her act wasn't fooling Karyn for a second. Serena thrived on excitement. As cool as she pretended to be, it had to be killing her to be sitting around with nothing to do. Nothing to do but sit around and eat grease.

"Do you advertise your services?" Karyn suggested.

It was the first day that Karyn was hanging out at the rented office space where Serena worked. Serena ignored the suggestion. She appreciated having Karyn around, but she wasn't going to change the way that she did business. She'd been doing just fine all these years, no need to make changes now.

"I'll take that as a 'no'. So what do we do?" Karyn asked, sincerely wanting to be helpful.

Serena dove into the last slice of pizza. With her mouth full, she said, "Nothing. Just wait for something to happen. It always does."

8

~~~Dad~~~

"I'm going back again." Jack told Elizabeth as he handed her a cup of coffee, just the way she liked it. He used a generous amount of milk and a ridiculous amount of sugar for Elizabeth's cup. It seemed like a waste of good coffee. Jack liked to grind the beans himself, making a wonderfully rich brew that gave the kitchen a heavenly aroma. Coffee was one of Jack's specialties and he usually drank it black.

"Thanks, honey, " she murmured, cupping the warm mug in her small hands. "Back?"

"To Virtual Memories." Jack said, amazed that Elizabeth didn't know what he was talking about.

"You liked it that much?" She peered at him over her steaming mug. The mug covered most of her face.

"It was something else! You've got to do it too." Jack stood with his feet spread widely apart, like a cowboy's stance. He bobbed his left knee with boyish excitement.

"Isn't it kind of expensive though?" Elizabeth crinkled up her face, forming what Jack lovingly called her "worry forehead".

"Well, I guess so, but it's worth it. Let's sign us both up." Jack's eyes sparkled with liquid energy. He was obviously not going to let go of this.

Elizabeth laughed. "OK, I'll do it. When do you want to go?"

Jack guiltily shifted his gaze. "Well, I already set up an appointment for me to go back. I made it for next Friday, if you don't mind. But you can go whenever you want." Jack drank his coffee, feeling like he was asking permission to go out. He resented that feeling.

He could never look Elizabeth in the face when he knew she would be miffed with something he'd done. Fridays were family days, the weekend. Jack never made plans for himself on Friday. Come to think of it, Jack was never *anywhere* without his family on the weekend. Not unless he had to work.

"Friday?" Elizabeth's eyebrows rose. "OK, I guess." Her "worry forehead" deepened.

"Maybe you'll go on Saturday?" Jack said with exaggerated brightness. This wasn't going over well.

"Maybe." Elizabeth scowled mournfully into her coffee.

The shrill blast of the kitchen phone startled Jack, who happened to be standing right next to it at the time. "Hello," he said curtly.

"That was fast," said a nasal voice, devoid of inflection or warmth. The voice conjured up an image of a droll little man, tubby and nerdish. It was pretty much an accurate picture.

"What's up?" Jack said without much enthusiasm. It was his older brother Vince, who seldom called. When he did call the conversations were never enjoyable.

"Mom wants to know if we will be there on Sunday." Vince got to the point right away. Heaven forbid he actually talk to his brother just to talk.

"Yeah, we'll be there. How is she?" Jack regretted that he'd forgotten to call her last night. He hoped his mother hadn't lain awake waiting for him to call.

"Not good. But what else is new?" Vince said, without detectable expression. The noise of a game on the TV was loud enough to be heard over the phone.

Vince's cold ways irritated Jack. Jack wasn't an overly sensitive man, but he sure was warmer than Vince. Vince seldom showed emotion, not even now, with their mother so ill.

His wife Sharon was colder, downright arctic. Ice ran in her veins. She didn't even like the company of her own children. The two as a couple made the room temperature drop a few degrees.

Ever since his mother had moved to the nursing home, Jack had seen way more of Vince and Sharon than he liked. Vince was the executor of her will, and he had a habit of discussing those sensitive matters as if they were talking about today's weather. He was as passionate as a dishrag. Limp, cold.

"We'll be there," Jack said again. It was his way of encouraging an end to this conversation. It worked.

"OK, I'll be seeing you." Vince didn't bother to wait for Jack to reply before he hung up the phone.

The Virtual Memories session was a perfect outlet for Jack's frustrations and his grief. It had been good to be home, back in time to when life was easier.

It was an excruciatingly painful waiting game with his mother. He wanted her to be at peace, free from the pain, and yet he could not bear to let her go. He knew she couldn't hang on much longer. The day of her passing would be difficult to bear.

He admired his mother, cherished her, and thought of her as one of his closest friends. She was a tender grandmother to his children, a good friend of his wife, and a loving person to all. Active in the community, she was always ready to volunteer or lend a hand. She would be missed in ways he could not fathom.

Jack could not bring himself to come to terms with her illness. He shut his ears when Elizabeth tried to discuss it with him. While he was at the hospital, he averted his eyes from seeing the various medical equipment that was keeping his mother alive. He was not going to deal with this until he was forced to.

Jack looked forward to his next session with a fever that went beyond an excitement over the extraordinary experience. He was sinking himself into it, thinking about the sessions obsessively.

He'd have to *plan* his session this time. He sure didn't want to waste his next session over something stupid like he did before, first watching himself sleeping and then freezing on a ski slope with some punk kid from his past whom he didn't even remember.

Jack knew the one person in his past he did want to see. His father. The man he'd lost when both men were much too young. With his mother so ill, Jack had been thinking about his dad a lot these days.

~~~Friday ~~~

Jack eagerly followed Smilin' Dan to the leather chair, impatiently grabbing the headset himself. He had the feeling he used to get as a kid at 10pm on Christmas Eve, knowing that Santa would come so soon that he could barely stand it.

"Jack, do you have a plan for how you would like to spend your second session? More high school memories?" Dan spoke with the lilting voice of someone who was a good listener. He was a hard person not to like.

"Well, sort of. I'd like to see my dad." Jack said.

"Has it been long since you've seen your father?" Dan asked carefully, accurately guessing that Jack's father was deceased.

"Yes, it's been over ten years. He died when I was about sixteen. Cancer." Jack didn't feel any pain in those words. It had been a long time.

"Ten years is a long time." Dan's voice was respectfully soft. His expression was kind, nearly angelic. An angel with a body worthy of Michaelangelo's paints.

"I'd like to see him again, hear him talk." Jack's stomach fluttered a little bit, nervous butterflies. After his first session, he expected that seeing his father would feel *real*. He couldn't imagine what it would be like to see his dad after all these years of longing to see his face, all these years of missing him.

"Select a day that you remember spending with your father. A holiday or a birthday?" Dan patted him on the upper back. "Enjoy your session, Jack. I hope you have the experience you are looking for." Dan stared at Jack for a lingering moment. His eyes communicated empathy.

Click!

Dan was out of the room and the lights were dim. Jack strained his eyes to adjust to the low light. He entered a date on the remote control. He didn't choose a holiday.

He didn't want to relive a special day. He

wanted a regular day. A day when everything was normal, when Dad was still alive, just a regular old day when Dad was there.

He entered a date at random, some summer day in 1983, before Dad was sick. His heart lurched as the memory came alive, flooding his senses instantaneously, overwhelmingly real.

It was the afternoon, an hour close to when he guessed that Dad would be home. He was inside the house, reading a book. The air was heavy with sweet pine. The house was warm, but a breeze traveled across the corn fields, intermittently entering the living room where Jack was sitting.

He'd forgotten the peace of the country and the safe feeling he had at home. Nothing bad could happen during a moment such as this.

He could hear his mother clanging the pans in the cabinet. A moment later the water was running. Spaghetti, thought Jack. He loved spaghetti.

He heard the unmistakable sound of gravel crunching under tires. *Dad!* He knew it had to be, it was his father coming home from work. Oh how he used to long for that sound! He never knew what such a sound would mean to him until he stopped hearing it.

The "Virtual Jack" stayed on the couch where he was sitting. *No, no! Get off that couch! Run to him! Run to him!* Jack thought in agony. He wanted to force the younger version of himself to stand up, to greet his father. To rush at him, hug him, touch him!

The car door slammed. Dad was home! He could hear his father approaching. He could hear his dress shoes clicking on the walk. He'd forgotten about his shoes and the sound that they'd made.

"Hi there, my son, my son," said a cheerful baritone. Dad was there, ruffling his hair. It was so real! He could feel his warm hand on his head, he could smell the lingering scent of his aftershave, he could feel the stiffness of his dress shirt as it brushed his cheek.

Oh Dad! It's you! Oh look at me, Dad! See my babies! I had two little girls, Dad. One looks just like you. My wife, you'd love her. Oh Dad, I've missed you so much! Jack cried out in anguish.

Virtual Jack said only "Hi, Dad."

His father left the living room for the kitchen, where he greeted Jack's mother. The smell of potatoes boiling filled the small house, he'd been wrong about the spaghetti.

Jack could hear his father's voice rise and fall. He was talking about his day. For the first time, Jack recognized *himself* in his dad. The familiar way he told a story, the excitement upon greeting his wife at the end of a long day. Like father, like son. Jack was mesmerized. He never realized how much he was like his father.

They sat together at the small round kitchen table, on wooden chairs covered with tie-down seat cushions. Jack, his parents and his sister. His brother was away at college.

Jack sank happily into his seat, across the table from his father. He was the first to dive into the steaming bowl of mashed potatoes in front of him. He watched butter melt into the creamy heap he put on his plate.

Dad was talking. His eyes were dancing with interest behind his glasses as he spoke. He said the family grace, a few short words. Then he continued to talk, as if there'd been no pause in conversation. He loaded his plate with steak, potatoes and corn with the same enthusiasm that Jack had shown.

His mother used the broiler to cook the steak, which left the kitchen hazy with smoke. The real Jack could feel the slight sting in his eyes from the smoke. He could smell that steak, and was salivating heavily. He lusted for the thick salty T-bone that Virtual Jack was cutting into.

Dad was talking about work. Jack savored every word, every expression. Dad wrinkled his nose, a subconscious gesture. He used his hands in exuberant sweeping motions while he spoke, not unlike the hand gestures of Jack's little girl, Dad's precious granddaughter. Oh how he would have adored Kimmie.

Oh Dad! Jack sobbed. *Tell me about religion, tell me about your work! Talk to me! I miss you! I want to hear all of your old war stories! I'm sorry I didn't listen. I don't remember what you said, tell me again, Dad, tell me again! Talk to me Dad! Dad, I'm right here! I'm right here! Dad, it's me! I want to be with you Dad!*

Jack broke down, buried his face in his hands and cried until there were no tears left. Sobs raked his body, making his lungs ache. He held his body, shaking uncontrollably. It was the first time he had really cried for his dad.

~~~ ~~~

Dan had entered the room when the session was over, but he quietly walked back out before Jack saw him. He allowed Jack to have a few moments of privacy to compose himself, then he returned to the room with a drink of water.

"I'm sorry you had a tough session, my friend," said the ever-compassionate muscle man. He squeezed Jack's shoulder. It seemed that Dan couldn't help but reach out to people physically when he was hurting for them emotionally. It was a style that Jack wasn't accustomed too, but one that he needed.

"It was excruciating. I couldn't interact. I couldn't do anything." Jack choked.

Dan gave Jack the water. "I thought you might be thirsty," he said awkwardly. He didn't want Jack to know that he'd seen him during his private moments of sorrow.

"I could only experience. I wanted to *do* something." His voice was thin and gravelly, barely above a whisper. He took a sip of the water.

"You *can* do something." Dan smiled. "The deluxe package is interactive."

"You mean I can make my past self do whatever I want?" Jack nearly shouted with glee, his breakdown already forgotten.

"Well, you can't change your past in *reality*, of course, but you can manipulate your memory, add fantasy to your memory, create a fictitious memory..."

"Are you serious?" Jack said, floored by the possibilities.

"Oh yes. But it's rather costly." Dan regretted baiting Jack. It wasn't something he did intentionally. But when he saw the raw pain in Jack's eyes he'd blurted out the first thing he thought of that could fix it. He knew Jack wasn't in the same league as the fantasy clients, it was out of his price range.

"*How* costly?" Jack was interested.

9

~~~Michelle~~~

Michelle marched into the Wilcox Detective Agency with the stride of someone who dared to be stopped. "I want to hire a private detective." She tossed her blond hair with a practiced shake of her head and squinted her eyes defiantly at Serena.

Serena was amused. She wondered how many hours this woman had spent in front of the mirror to get that little hair toss thing down to a science. "Why do you need a detective?"

Michelle frowned with her pouty made up lips. "I think my husband is messing around on me or something." She rolled her eyes dramatically.

"Ah, I see." Serena stood away from her mammoth sized oak desk and extended her hand to

Michelle. "Serena Wilcox, and you are?"

"Michelle," she said tersely. Her blue leather jacket and coordinating mini skirt mummified her body. None of her womanly curves were left to the imagination. The matching blue stilettos were muddied from the spring muck, a detail that Serena had gleefully noticed.

"Take a seat and tell me what you want us to do." She gestured toward a high backed burgundy chair across from her own leather desk chair.

Serena was wearing her work clothes, a brown polar fleece oversized sweatshirt with coordinating brown leggings. At home she wore sweats. She dressed in expensive business suits on occasion, but those occasions were seldom.

Serena enjoyed wearing dresses, jewelry and makeup, but didn't bother to wear them very often. It took too much time. Why spend an hour getting ready for the day, when she could spend that hour sleeping in?

Serena *couldn't* look sloppy. With her childlike face and petite body, no matter what she wore, she always managed to look perky, cute.

"Perky" was a word Serena hated, wishing instead to appear as sharp and sophisticated as she knew herself to be. Why couldn't she have been born taller? Serena wore vertical stripes as often as she could to look less short, and less round.

Michelle sat, swiftly crossing her legs. *She* was tall, very. Her legs seemed to stretch endlessly, long limbs of toned flesh. She sat in such a way as to make others very aware of her physical assets. Being seductive was a habit with her. It was no longer a conscious decision.

Michelle pulled out a stick of gum, unwrapped it and started chewing it like a cow chewing on its cud. The wrapper was poised in her slender fingers.

"OK then, what do you want us to do?" Serena said in her professional voice. She held a small trash can out for Michelle to drop her gum wrapper into.

"I want you to look into a place called Virtual Memories." Michelle came close to smiling, showing off the results of good dentistry.

"The fancy computer game?" Serena's curiosity was piqued.

"Yeah, I guess. I want to know what my husband is doing there. When he goes there, what he does." Michelle said, bored by their discussion.

"You think he's meeting someone there?" Serena was certain that Michelle was holding back something, but what? And why was she so dispassionate if she suspected her husband of having an affair?

"Yeah, maybe. I want to know why he goes there." Michelle was on her feet, staring wistfully at the door. She chomped on the gum, moving her jaws with vigor, creating a smacking noise that annoyed Serena greatly.

"We charge a flat fee for..." Serena began.

Michelle waved her hand, a hand meticulously manicured. "Bill me. I don't care what it costs."

Serena arched one eyebrow. She shrugged. "OK. What's your husband's name?"

"Jack." Michelle said, exhaling a steamy breath that smelled like cinnamon gum. She laughed for no apparent reason, a bitter cackle that wreaked of vindictiveness.

"Jack?"

"Jack Miller." Michelle tossed his business card on Serena's desk.

Serena glanced at the card. It would be enough information to work with. "How can I reach you?"

Michelle tugged at the bottom of her leather skirt, wriggling until the skirt was smooth. She leaned over Serena's desk unexpectedly, waving the wad of wet gum toward her astonished face.

"Here, hold this a sec." She snapped.

Serena was so startled by the request that she just did as she was asked. She held the lipstick stained gum as far from her face as she could. *I am such a weenie*, she thought.

Michelle tugged at the bottom of the leather jacket, smoothing out the folds. She held a pen in her mouth while she dug into her purse for a piece of paper. She scribbled down her phone number and placed it on the desk.

Then she snatched her gum from Serena's outstretched hand and popped it into her mouth. "There. You've got my phone number now. Call me when you have something."

10

~~~Elizabeth's Session~~~

"So I can re-live any day I want?" Elizabeth studied the remote control warily. Jack dropped her off at Virtual Memories and took the girls to the Burger King play area, leaving her here to play a game they couldn't afford. "The training video..."

"Video?" Stewart Lamont drew attention to Elizabeth's inaccuracies with a robust snort. The *video*! That was the trouble with women, they took the best things of man and reduced them down to the ordinary.

The training session was an exquisite computer programming work of *art*, it was *no* video. *That's what happens when you let women think for themselves*, he thought piggishly. His eyes panned over Elizabeth's chest. *Women were good for only one thing.*

"The virtual training session, whatever you call it." Elizabeth said dismissively. Inside she was simmering. She called the training session by the wrong name, big deal, she was *nervous.* It didn't mean she was *stupid.* Stewart set Elizabeth's teeth on edge, especially that obnoxious slurping on hard candy. *What a pervert,* she thought.

"The introduction to our services, given by your Virtual Guide." Lamont corrected her. His eyes flicked over Elizabeth's legs. "What part of the tutorial didn't you understand?"

Elizabeth tried to ignore his patronizing tone, what did *she* care what he thought of her? If they did an IQ comparison, she knew she'd blow him out of the murky sewer he swam in. The tutorial wasn't very detailed, it wasn't a problem of low comprehension on her part.

If he wanted to live in denial, that he, a man, was intellectually superior to all women, she wasn't going to be the one to break the news to him. Most women were not only smarter than this dolt, but they could see right through his rat-infested head.

Her Virtual Guide had been the "Virtual Lamont", who was no more appealing than the live version. Elizabeth grimaced at the reminder. Why couldn't she have had that Dan guy that Jack talked about? She should have spoken up when she first realized she was stuck with Lamont.

"The Guide didn't say anything about being able to fast forward. I don't want to waste time on things I don't care about. Can I skip ahead to find what I am looking for?" Elizabeth asked. She felt creepy sitting in the purple room. It was too weird.

Skipping ahead was a question Jack hadn't thought to ask when he had his first session. It would have saved him a lot of time. He could have used the fast forward option to skip past the parts of his session where he was sleeping, instead of helplessly falling into a sluggish state, wasting his session time.

Lamont popped a cherry candy into his mouth, annoyed. "Yeah, sure, just use the same arrow that you use to scan the dates."

"OK, thanks." Elizabeth said as sweetly as she could muster.

"Ready now?" He said, staring at her. She reminded him of his sister, the superacheiving Class Treasurer. He despised her, and all women like her.

"I think so." *Please go*, she thought. The tension between them was like a block of cold lard. Thick and greasy. He reminded her of her first boyfriend, the womanizer. She despised him, and all men like him.

"OK, catch ya on the other side, " Lamont said in a parting phrase that *he* no doubt thought was witty. When Elizabeth didn't respond to his clever turn of phrase, he assumed she didn't comprehend it.

Click!

The lights dimmed. *Thank God he's out of here*, she thought. She shivered, trying to shake off the willies from his hands on her face when he was adjusting the headset and goggles. She felt his maleness hard against her as he leaned over her body. *Disgusting!* She tried to put the image behind her, never to be recalled again, she hoped. *GAG!*

Within seconds, Elizabeth had forgotten about Lamont. During her training session she was overpowered by the sights, sounds— even the smells of the virtual experience. And the touch! She could really *feel* things! It was incredible, just like Jack said, *absolutely incredible*. She quickly forgave him for his boyish obsession with this place.

Elizabeth knew exactly which date to visit. Unlike Jack, she had her session planned from the first appointment, so she dove right in to the session. She pressed her chosen date into the remote control keypad and pressed 'enter'.

Vvroom!

The memory rushed at her, filling her senses instantly, and overwhelmingly. The sudden intensity of the light momentarily blinded her. Simultaneously, the smell of antiseptic engulfed her like an invisible fog. The odor frightened her. *Stark fear*.

She could hear the distinct electronic sound that was her lifeline, the *bleep, bleep, bleep* of the fetal heart monitor machine. She was alone in the small white room, but the din in the hall assured her that the nursing staff was close by. She was aware that her doctor was being paged.

She heard a small groan coming from deep inside the Virtual Elizabeth. She felt those sound vibrations coming from her own throat, as she watched her past self from the comfort of a leather lounger. She saw her own head turn toward the bleeping noises. She was stunned by how real it all was.

A jagged line peaked across a roll of paper coming from the machine, charting a particularly powerful contraction. The real Elizabeth felt no physical pain. Yet she *could* feel it.

She was cold and shaking. Somehow she could experience the *sensation* of the pain, as if she were having a dream about it. She was aware of the pain. She could recognize it happening.

She didn't hurt from it, not like the Virtual Elizabeth was feeling it now. But just like in a nightmare, the real Elizabeth smelled *raw fear*, and understood what was happening to her physical self. She watched her past self, horrified that she could do nothing to help.

The Virtual Elizabeth was fretful, she was rolling from side to side, holding her breath. She had abandoned the breathing exercises she'd learned in Lamaze class.

Breathe, she told herself. *Not much longer.* You can *do* this, you *did* do this.

A nurse hurried to her side. Her soft bosom pressed up against Elizabeth's neck as she reached across her to arrange a pillow under her side, kindly trying to make her more comfortable. The nurse seemed like an angel, a woman whose face she had long forgotten, but who now seemed so familiar to her.

"Your doctor is on his way in," she said. She patted Elizabeth's arm. "It won't be long now." The woman's eyes were those of a mother looking down at her sleeping baby. Elizabeth made a mental note to do something nice for this veteran nurse.

Jack was suddenly right beside her, grabbing her arm. He'd been asleep in the lounge, with their firstborn daughter Kimmie. He didn't know that things were starting to happen until the nurse woke him up.

Elizabeth had *encouraged* him to take Kimmie, and go to sleep *in the lounge*. He'd been falling asleep right there in her room. The sight of him sleeping, unable to keep his eyes open to see her through the night, infuriated her. But she didn't want to skip ahead. Even this part of her birthing experience seemed precious to her.

She had been so angry looking at his body dozing in the chair, that she wanted him OUT. *Sleep somewhere else. So I can concentrate on finding peace in my pain, and not have to look at you — sleeping through my most hellish moments!*

He'd come back in the room, just in time for Elizabeth to start pushing. He held one knee. The nurse held the other. They encouraged her to push. She felt separate from Jack at that moment, still angry that he could sleep when she was so afraid, and in such pain.

The baby's head had gone back up, the bottom just under her ribs, after she had been dilated 4 cm for over two weeks. When the doctor decided to admit her and break her water, there was some risk involved. The baby's head was too far up. Jack could *sleep* during the fretful waiting?

But when she finally surrendered, and looked at Jack, she saw only the unconditional love of a man who cherished his wife and unborn child. His blue eyes held her, stilled her. The anger left her. Jack was her soulmate. *And he was here.*

She could do this. It would be OK. Soon they would have their beautiful new baby. Her husband's strength touched her every fiber of being. She needed him. She was relieved that he was there.

Pushing was a sensation like no other. Some describe it like the muscular contractions needed to have a bowel movement, which Elizabeth thought was the closest comparison, but there was really *no* way to accurately explain what it felt like to push a baby out of the womb. There was no other experience like it.

Elizabeth would never forget what it felt like, never *want* to forget. Her labor was so personal, *so heartwrenching*. She had visited this moment in her mind countless times, but never was it as real as this, *the virtual memory* of the day Hannah was born, far more intense than a mere memory. She had traveled back in time to this precious moment: In spirit, and to some extent, in body.

Virtual Elizabeth was crunching forward, folding her body toward her knees. She could see the worry on the nurses' faces. She wondered if something was going wrong.

Jack was alert, still holding her leg, and telling her, "I see the head, it's right there. One more push. *One more push, honey.*" Elizabeth could feel Jack's firm, yet gentle, pressure on her thigh. It steadied her.

It was she and Jack. Like always. She could do this.

A chorus of "One more push" arose from the medical staff and Jack, whose voice rose above the others in Elizabeth's mind. The Virtual Elizabeth seemed stronger at that moment, as she gave the final push. In an eye's blink, the doctor had slipped the baby out, and onto her belly.

Tears streamed down the real Elizabeth's face as she watched herself reach out for Hannah. The baby's eyes were squeezed shut like a fisted hand — until Elizabeth spoke.

"Hi baby," she said. Hannah's delicate lids opened. First a tiny slit, then wider. Elizabeth could see the dark shining pools of her newborn baby's eyes.

The real Elizabeth reached her hand out toward the image before her. She could feel the rose-petal softness of the baby's skin. She felt the downy hairs on Hannah's tiny limbs. Her sweet hazy newborn scent filled her nose. She drank it all in, savoring it to return to later, in her memories.

Elizabeth used the remote control to fast forward over the next few minutes, until she found what she was looking for: the image of herself nursing Hannah for the first time.

Hannah's silky pink lips opened, searching for her momma's breast. The baby's tiny mouth seemed too small for the large mother's breast pressing into the newborn's face, but the baby latched on to the nipple right away, as if mother and baby knew each other long before birth.

Nursing was much easier the second time around. She didn't have the same frustrations she'd had with Kimmie. Hannah nursed easily, a natural transition from womb to breast.

Virtual Elizabeth smiled lovingly at the baby, stroking the side of Hannah's cheek. The baby fell asleep within seconds. The smell of her milky sleepbreath was so real, so poignant.

The real Elizabeth felt her breasts tighten, as if they were letting down to nurse. She looked down at her blouse, but could not see it in the darkness of the room.

She knew it was damp. How could this be? Hannah was weaned weeks ago. Elizabeth hadn't had any leaking since.

How embarrassing. *I must have gotten too emotional*, she thought.

Click!

The lights came up as her session's time ran out. When Lamont returned, he openly stared at her wet blouse. It made Elizabeth's skin crawl.

Get me out of here, she silently screamed.

11

~~~George~~~

George Bowmann picked up the phone. It was his kid sister Janet. George groaned. *Now* he could put a name to that nagging feeling he'd been having lately, it was guilt. Shoot. How could he have forgotten to call her back? "Janie, I meant to get back with you..."

"Oh don't worry about it, I know how you are." Janie's voice smiled through the phone line.

Janet was a sweet girl, naive and full of hope. Even after going through some tough times, she was still a Catholic school girl wearing plaid dresses and exchanging whispered giggles with her girlfriends. To George, she'd *always* be that little girl.

"Hey!" George snorted. "What's that

supposed to mean?" His voice was playful, a rare sound in the office. *I need to get out more*, he thought.

"Only that you *never* return my calls." Janet said in an exaggerated whine. She could never stay mad at her big brother, the man whom she measured all other men against.

"I wouldn't say 'never'." George said, reaching for his glasses. He took his glasses on and off all day, off when the weight of his frames on his sinuses gave him a headache, and back on when he wanted to see again. His vision was so poor, he really should consider buying contact lenses, or get lighter frames.

"Never." Janet said emphatically.

"Really?" George teased. He knew she was right. He'd been preoccupied with work since the day he was born. He wasn't much of a people person.

But he enjoyed hearing from Janet. He didn't deliberately dodge her calls. Somehow, time always had a way of slipping away from him.

"Yes. But that's OK. We know how you are," said Janet, not unkindly, but with the resignation of a sibling who knew her brother well.

"OK, OK, message received. So how are you and the baby doing?" George tapped a pencil on the edge of his desk. It was an expensive mechanical pencil. The lead broke from the vigorous rapping. *Aargh!* It was the third lead he had broken that day.

"Fine. Sadie is sitting up on her own now." Janet's voice was soft, mellow. She was stroking the baby's downy cheek as she spoke. The baby was asleep, curled up in her mother's lap.

"Great," he said. George entered some data into the computer. It was a file he was working on when the phone rang and it had been staring him in the face while he talked.

"George, do I hear you typing something?" Janet said, her voice accusatory.

"How's the new husband?" George stopped typing.

"Tom is working nights this week, but he doesn't seem to mind it." Janet sighed, an exaggerated sound for her brother's benefit. "I notice you ignored my question."

George laughed. "OK you caught me. But I am listening to you, really."

"I was calling to remind you that we are throwing Mom a surprise birthday party." Janet said cheerily. She and the rest of the family had been working on the party plans for months. George's schedule had kept him too busy to lend a hand. She wondered if he even remembered where the party was going to be held.

"Oh, yeah, when is that again?" He said, aware that his admission of such ignorance would irritate Janet.

"Oh *George!* It's—"

blip blip

"That's not your call waiting, is it?" said Janie in exasperation.

"Yeah, it'll just be a minute." George could almost *hear* Janet's eyes rolling, expressing her annoyance.

He switched to the second caller. "Bowmann."

"George? It's Serena Wilcox." Serena sounded muffled. Was the woman eating something?

"Serena who?" George mused.

"I met you while working on the in-vitro scam case."

"I was joking. Of course I remember you." George ran his hand through his hair. The woman intrigued him.

"I have a question for you." Serena made a smacking sound with her lips.

"Are you eating something?" George hoped he made her blush.

"Pizza." She didn't sound like she was blushing.

"Thought so."

"My question?" Serena said firmly.

"Shoot."

"A woman hires me to investigate her husband, but when I do a check on her I find out that she's not married to him."

"She's lying?"

"Yeah. I don't know why." Serena dabbed at the corners of her pretty heart-shaped lips with a washcloth. She was out of paper napkins.

"Isn't it your job to find out?" George crossed his arms smugly, phone cradled in his neck.

"Yeah, yeah. I wanted to know if you wanted in on this case," Serena offered casually, yet with a note of something else in her voice.

George leaned forward onto his elbow. "What would you need *me* for?"

Click

"What was that?" Serena asked. She wondered if George was taking another call. She hoped he wasn't.

"My sister was on the other line. She hung up." He said. Yikes, he was in trouble with the family now. *George the jerk.* Oh well, he'd worn *that* title before.

"Which sister?" Serena asked, genuinely interested. She liked his family, such a large family of nice sharp people. She didn't know how his mother did it. All those kids under one roof! Of course they were all grown now. But the grandchildren probably kept her running.

"Janet." George said impatiently. He resumed typing at the keyboard. That open file was staring him in the face, begging him to work on it. He seldom took personal calls at work.

"Oh, what did she have?" Serena said, taking a sip of her soda. She was not in a hurry. Was Serena *ever* in a hurry?

"A girl. Named her Sadie." George typed faster, ignoring the crick in his neck from cradling the phone under his chin. If Serena noticed the distinct sound of him *working*, she sure didn't acknowledge it.

"Ah, how nice. Did she get married?"

"Last month."

"That's nice."

"Listen, Serena, I have stuff to do. What do you need me for?" His voice was gruff, irritated. It was his cool working-with-impossible-clients voice. He felt a fleeting twinge of guilt from using this tone with Serena, the pixie faced detective.

"I don't know yet." Serena didn't sound at all affected by his "cool" tone. She was the type of woman who seldom let on when she felt offended by others. She didn't like confrontations or awkward conversations. She liked things to be *nice*.

George sighed noisily. "What did you call for?"

"To see if I can count on your help if I need it."

"Yeah, count me in. Now go eat your pizza and let me work."

"I'll call you."

"Yeah, yeah, later." George hung up. That woman really got to him. Good or bad, he didn't know.

12

~~~Jack's Fantasy Session~~~

"Jack, I don't understand why you want to spend $1,000 on this." Elizabeth was wearing her worry forehead again. It was becoming her daily look.

"*You* had a session." His eyes darted to meet hers, daring her to argue with him.

"It was fantastic, but *look at me*! Ever since I did it I've been leaking breast milk. I am going to have to go to the doctor if it doesn't stop." Her blouse was damp. It was her third shirt of the day and it wasn't even noon.

"OK, I admit that's a little weird, but you don't know for sure that it had anything to do with your session." Jack raised his eyebrows in an expression that Elizabeth knew to mean: I have a weak case, and I know it, but I am gonna argue with you anyway.

"Oh give me a break. Of *course* it was because of the session! I wasn't leaking until right after the session was ending. I feel like a freak."

"I haven't had anything like that happen. This could be a hormonal thing."

"I think it's a reaction to that Memory Something chocolate drink."

"Memory Enhancing Shake." Jack said grudgingly. He doubted there was anything to her paranoia. Hormones. It's not like she didn't have trouble with hormones before.

"Whatever. I'm not sure if it's safe to keep doing this, Jack." Elizabeth hesitated before adding the second point in her argument, knowing that she was opening herself up to a deeper fight. "And for $1,000? We can't afford that!"

"And *whose* fault is that?" Jack glared at her. He leaned arrogantly against the counter, daring her to tangle with him. They weren't the loving couple at this moment, but players on opposing teams.

Elizabeth blinked, stunned. "*What?*"

"You heard me." Jack said with a nonchalance that mocked her. He was pushing this to ugly levels.

Elizabeth slammed her hand on the table, ignoring the smart pain that radiated up her arm. "I can't believe you just said that!" She snapped, her eyes firing back at him.

Jack didn't respond.

"I put off finishing college to marry you. By the time I had my chance to go back, I had a baby to take care of. Then I helped you get *your* career off the ground. Now, I am trying to work while being home with the girls. How *dare* you blame me for our family income!" Elizabeth shook from built up resentment. Her fingernails bit into the palms of her hands.

Jack stared back at her, a snide smile across his lips. The sight of his face made Elizabeth's own grow hot.

The two studied each other, the air charged with their energy. I am not going to give him the satisfaction of provoking me, thought Elizabeth. "I can't believe you just said that."

She let her voice drop, showing her resignation. The two knew each other like childhood friends. Jack knew that her "resignation" meant that she was going to stew about this for days, and then *really* let him have it later, at the most inconvenient moment. Maybe right as they were going out the door. Maybe just as he was about to fall asleep at night.

"Jack do whatever you want, it's your money." She said, shrugging. This gesture didn't fool him for a second. Nope, the wife was pissed. He'd be dealing with this for a long time.

"You know I support you." Jack said flippantly, digging himself further into his self-made hole. He was irritated with himself for opening the financial can of worms.

"Then why is it that *every* time we have an argument you bring up the fact that I am not working?" Elizabeth's voice was soft, fearful.

Jack sighed. He wasn't in the mood for this. "I don't know. Because it gets to you I guess."

"You say it *deliberately to hurt me?*" Elizabeth

said theatrically. She opened her hands while she spoke, the tension beginning to let up. She was tired of the fight.

"Sort of. I don't care what you do." Jack felt his foot in his mouth and corrected himself, "You know what I mean, I support you finding work from home. You'll make it. I'm just mad because you are getting all pissy about me going to the session. You were the one who started me on it in the first place."

Elizabeth laughed. They sounded ridiculous squabbling like chickens. She hated it when Jack thought of her as a nagging shrew. She got 'pissy'? *No, I don't think so!*

But, this wasn't something she was willing to lose sleep over. She decided to let it go. She was tired and had other things on her mind, was it really worth getting so upset over this?

Whew, thought Jack. *Fight over*. He could tell by his wife's expression that, for some reason that wasn't clear to him, she was dropping the argument. For now anyway.

"Well I didn't count on you getting hooked on it." Elizabeth said gently, wary that the fighting would pick up right where they left off.

Jack shrugged. "It's fun. It's not like I go to bars or anything."

"Do you *want* to be going to bars?" Elizabeth asked. What *was* this? Was Jack not happy at home? She didn't trap him here, he voluntarily came home to her and the girls. Did he resent coming home every night? What was up with this? She felt a trickle of fear, an anxiety that would become a familiar feeling over the next few days.

"No Elizabeth, that's not what I meant. I

mean, why should you get mad if I do this?" Jack was more annoyed than reassuring to Elizabeth's ears. He just didn't have the heart for this conversation today.

"$1,000 is a lot of money, besides I was hoping we'd do something fun on the weekend. Those sessions take up the whole afternoon." Elizabeth quickly added, "But I'll deal with it if you really want to do it."

"Yeah, I want to do it, if you don't mind." Jack said, with no warmth in his voice. His eyes looked away from Elizabeth. It was his signal that he wanted the conversation to be over.

"Jack, you *know* I mind. But do what you want." Elizabeth hated being disagreeable. And Jack wasn't backing down. What choice did she have, other than be a shrew? She vowed never to tell Jack what he can and cannot do. She was his wife, his friend. Not his mother.

"OK, I'll go." Jack smiled and kissed the top of his wife's head.

Elizabeth tried to squelch her anger. It wasn't such a big deal, right? She was just being insecure, she chided herself. But why did she have that dreaded nagging feeling of impending doom, that these sessions were a bad thing, something that could tear them apart? She shivered, trying to shake off her own fears.

"Liz, I just can't tell you how good it was to see Dad again. I know I haven't really talked about it much, but I will. Just give me time." Jack gave her shoulders an affectionate squeeze.

"This is something you really want?" Elizabeth asked, already knowing the answer.

"Yes, it is. It's something that I need right now." Jack kissed her on the cheek. He couldn't stop her from worrying, but hopefully he was out of the dog house.

~~~ ~~~

Jack greeted Dan with enthusiasm. "Dan, my man, I am ready for you today!" He bounced down the corridor toward the door that was now familiar to him.

Dan laughed. "OK, let's get to it then!"

Jack sank into the leather chair, left knee bobbing in restless anticipation. "So what do I do?"

"We'll let you look at a series of disks. There are scenarios you can choose from. We can start with general categories, such as the subjects found in your local video store." Dan said, giving Jack a full color brochure to leaf through.

Dan enjoyed this part of the job. It was interesting to see what kind of fantasy clients wanted. Sometimes Dan was able to guess what they would go for, other times he was way off. He was banking on Jack being the adventure type.

Virtual Memories didn't allow porn or obscene fantasies, which was a relief. Some of his clients were strange people. Dan could only imagine what kind of twisted virtual sessions they'd choose.

He hoped that Virtual Memories would be

alone in this technology for a long, long time. Eventually greed would create a market for the unscrupulous, but at least for now, they were able to run a class act.

Virtual Memories even had a policy stating that any clients who create a fantasy in which they perform a criminal act should be reported to authorities. Dan appreciated keeping the business clean. He hoped it would remain that way, but rumor had it that they would have a change in top level management soon. Anything could happen then.

"So, like comedies or action, like that?" Jack's eyes sparkled.

"Yep, we have four categories: Adventure, Comedy, Horror and Romance. You can pick one of the four, then I can let you browse through the disks until you make a selection."

"Cool! So it's like a live movie in my head?" Jack opened the brochure, skimming over the descriptions as fast as his eyes could read.

"Yeah, that's the perfect way to describe it. It will feel very real to you, and you will be the main character in the story. You'll have your choice of who will play the secondary characters." Dan opened his snappy leather briefcase to find another brochure for Jack to read.

"How do I choose that?" Jack said, reaching for the second brochure.

"There's another disk, a character disk, with photos of people that work for Virtual Memories. You can select which of these characters you want to incorporate into your fantasy session. You can even bring me a disk with photos of your family or friends on it if you'd rather." So far only one of Dan's clients had gone for that option, bringing in files of his dog.

"Nah, I'll stick with whatever you have. I don't want to bother making my own disk." So as not to offend Dan, Jack quickly added, "It's a cool idea though."

Jack suspected that Dan was personally disappointed when people didn't respond to all Virtual Memories' dazzling technological options with an eagerness to try them all. He wasn't far off in his impression. Dan did feel somewhat rejected when his clients passed on something he thought was incredible.

Dan took a chart and a pen from his tidy briefcase. Even his briefcase had the Virtual Memories logo on it, embossed into the leather. "So today we can get your fantasy all set up, and then we can schedule a session for you."

"I can't do it today?" Jack's voice dripped with his disappointment. He was all psyched up to do this. Elizabeth wouldn't be too thrilled to learn that he was coming back for yet another appointment at Virtual Memories.

"I'm sorry, I thought I had explained that to you. It takes a while to program the fantasy, customizing it with your selections." Dan said carefully. He tried not to sound defensive, but he sure hated it when clients had unrealistic expectations of what they could do. The sessions were so utterly fantastic, you'd think they'd understand that it takes a little bit of preparation.

"OK, I understand. Are these my options here?" Jack pointed to the list of storylines to choose from in each of the categories.

"Yes, you select one of the categories, and a

storyline. Then look at the other brochure to pick out the characters for your story. You can always opt to add the characters later, during your session. Some of the storylines have that option." Dan said. He was telling Jack everything that he could actually read for himself if he took the time to read through all the literature in the brochure.

Jack didn't bother to read the information. "How about going with 'Adventure'."

"Sure. I'll get you the Adventure Disk Pack. You can choose which story you like, the setting you want the story to take place in, and the characters you want in the story, based on the profiles in the Character Disk summary." Dan left the room, hoping that Jack would read through the material while he was out.

Jack read the possible storylines. He chose the one called "The Pursuit". He had his choice of "city", "fictional" or "unknown" setting. He chose "unknown". He checked the box next to "Choose characters during session".

Dan returned with a vinyl case that contained the Adventure Disk Pack. The soles of his shoes squealed as they hit the floor. "Oops, sorry about these shoes. My girlfriend talked me into getting these." Dan frowned at the shiny brown loafers in question.

"A new girlfriend?" Jack was amused.

"Yes, met her about two weeks ago, when she came in to ask about getting a session. Then I bumped into her again at the gym right after I got off work, so we started talking and we hit it off right away."

"Why did you have to mention the gym?

Makes me feel like an old fat guy when you do that!" Jack grinned.

"You oughta come out and lift with me, lose that old fat guy," Dan said hopefully. He liked Jack.

"Nah, too busy, too tired." Jack said dismissively.

"Maybe I'll get you to come around. Did you make your selections?" Dan asked, changing the subject. He noticed that weight and fitness were touchy subjects for Jack.

"Yep, got it all filled out." He gave Dan his completed form.

"This is the Adventure Pack. See, it's a bunch of data stored on CD's. We'll add the personalization for you before your session." Dan said, happy to be finished with his last client of the day.

"Great! I'm looking forward to it!" Jack followed Dan to the lobby area.

"Have a good evening, Jack."

"You too." Jack waved with two fingers on his way out the double glass doors.

13

~~~Wilcox Detective Agency~~~

Karyn stood in front of Serena's desk with her hands on her hips. She sniffed, pouting. "You mean I finally don't bother to come in, after sitting around doing *nothing* all week, and I miss the whole thing?"

"Well, it's wasn't that big of a thing. She was here for all of ten minutes maybe." Serena slurped her generously sweetened coffee.

She called Karyn after Michelle left, filling her in on that strange meeting. This would be their first case together. Karyn sure was eager to get started. She was at the office within ten short minutes.

Serena hoped that Karyn wouldn't be too disappointed, it wasn't likely that the case would develop into much. Odds were, they wouldn't find anything as exciting as what their own imaginations could conjure up. Serena wondered if she had done the right thing in teaming up with Karyn. Did she really need a partner?

"So what do we do?" Karyn laughed.

Well, thought Serena, *if nothing else, it's good to have a friend around. Sure beats sitting in this office by myself.*

Aloud she said, "We start looking into Jack Miller's life."

Karyn sank into a chair and folded her legs in a yoga-like position. "But why would we do that if we know she's lying about being married to him?"

"Because she asked us to." Serena said simply.

"We work for anybody that comes along?" Karyn studied Serena's face. She never knew what her friend might say. But whatever came out of her mouth was sure to be interesting.

"No, I never work for the bad guy." Serena said, miffed. She always took the high road. If she ever got to the point where she needed money so badly that her only choice was to aid a sleezy client, she would find another line of work.

"OK. So why are we working for this Michelle person?" Karyn raised her eyebrows. She observed that Serena had a pen in hand. She was hopeful that they had work to do.

"Because I think there's another client in it." Serena scribbled on a memo pad. Her face was scrunched in concentration, hand busy writing. Karyn strained to see what Serena was writing. She saw nothing but doodles of odd cartoon faces.

"I don't get why we are doing this." Karyn

studied the doodles. Not half bad, funny. Artistic talent, what do you know? She learned something new about Serena every day.

"Let's say we do what Michelle says, and we come across something interesting. We can offer our services to someone more worthy of our help." Serena drew a picture of a voluptuous woman with full lips and a snide facial expression. Karyn guessed it was a caricature of Michelle. A Cruella DeVille with curves and tighter clothes.

"We can do that? Work against our own client?" Karyn wondered what the rules were. Did they *have* rules? What was their job anyway?

"When we finish the job for Michelle she will be our *ex*-client. We have to trust that our new client doesn't go spreading it around how he or she came across hiring us." Serena said thoughtfully.

She tore off the doodle sheet and tossed it into the trash can beside her desk. She missed, leaned over, picked it up, and threw it again. This time the crumpled ball made it into the trash.

"Ah. But what if there's nothing to this story?" Karyn worried. She wondered if this was exactly legal. Karyn was the type who didn't go over the speed limit. She had a fear of authority, even though she had absolutely no reason to. When she had been a child, teachers often made remarks addressed to her entire class such as "I am disappointed with your behavior, you need to work harder." Karyn often took the "you" very personally, and did work harder. She fretted about the lecture, unaware that her teacher was not talking about her at all.

"We'll find out." Serena shrugged. Serena had been the type of child who probably *should* have been listening when teachers made lectures to the class.

"So what you're saying is, we are doing what she wants? At least for now?" Karyn said.

"Yep. We'll follow Jack Miller around, look into who he is and what he does." Serena started a new doodle. "I already looked into Virtual Memories. I gave her a call about that, she seemed pleased."

"What did you say to her?" Karyn regretted missing all of this. Things were finally starting to happen, and she was at home playing online.

"I told her that Jack Miller was scheduling sessions with an employee named Dan, and that he was becoming a regular player of the Virtual games, whatever those things are."

"Yeah I don't get that whole Virtual thing either. She sounded happy about that? I wonder why." Karyn had no idea what this woman's game could be.

"I think she wanted to know if Jack was a regular player, and who had him as a client." Serena stopped doodling. "I think she was happy that Jack is becoming a regular player, but I don't know why."

"That's more than I would have picked up on, you work fast." Karyn was impressed.

"It was easy information to find. It took one phone call. She could have gotten it herself actually. Makes me think that they know her at Virtual Memories." Serena said. She drank her coffee, which was now cold.

"How did you figure all of that out?" asked Karyn.

"I mostly use deductive reasoning."

"You mean you 'guess'?"

"I'm seldom wrong." Serena grinned. "Michelle already knew that Jack was going to Virtual Memories. She was fishing for more information. She was satisfied with what I gave her, so it must have been what she wanted to know."

"Michelle wants us to continue following Jack even though she already got what she wanted?" Karyn asked, with a hunch that she knew what Serena was up to.

"She hasn't *told* me to stop looking into it." Serena said slyly.

"OK, boss lady. I'll do whatever you say." Karyn gave her a little salute.

14

~~~Dan's Apartment~~~

"It's fascinating how that fantasy stuff works." Dan's new girlfriend said lazily. She gazed at Dan's broad muscular back and lightly touched his shirt with the tip of one long manicured nail.

"Yes, it's interesting work." Dan flushed from her physical closeness to him. He wasn't sure what to think of her, but he was trying to keep an open mind.

He wasn't impressed with the seduction routine. And yet, she was smart and funny. They had hit it off right away. She was giving off mixed signals of class meets tack. One minute she was coming on to him like a cat in heat, the next she was surprising him with clever conversation. Like the interest she had in his job with Virtual Memories.

"So you have to program all of the characters?" She leaned her full bosom into his back, pressing herself so close to him that he could smell the hair spray she had used that morning.

"Yeah, the clients select what they want and then I program it all in. It's not that difficult, the software is all set up to just plug everything in." Dan nodded his head toward the computer. "I just add the picture files when it prompts me to do that. The program does the rest."

His girlfriend smiled in interest. "You do it right here in your apartment?" She looked thoughtfully at the computer.

"Well, yeah. I'd rather do it home than hang around the office." Dan said. "I'm there all the time."

"I wish I could work at home, that would be great. No more waking up at 6 A.M. and driving in any weather. Especially when the roads are bad," she said wistfully.

"Oh, I wish I could work at home too. But most of my work involves running the programs for my clients, and showing them how to use it. Setting up their choices, putting the package together." Dan scowled, realizing just how much of his life was consumed with work. "I put in a full eight hours at Virtual. Then I come home and program for another three or four hours."

"So whatever you program is what the fantasy plays?" She asked. She was staring at the computer, even though it was not turned on.

"Um, yeah, sort of. It's not up to me though, I just put in what the client asks for." Dan booted up the computer, thinking how it was odd that she changed the subject as if she wasn't listening to him. "I can show you real quick."

"Oh could you? I'd like to see it." She flipped her blond hair off her shoulders, spraying the air with a musky mix of expensive shampoo and perfume.

"Yeah, I just open the client's file..." Dan brought up a menu of the clients assigned to him. He highlighted a name from the list, someone named Kim Brown. Kim's file came up.

"That's pretty neat. So what do you do now?" She slid next to him in the desk chair. There really wasn't room for both of them, so she curled up over one of his legs.

"I can get you a chair." Dan said, hoping she wouldn't put up a fuss. It was awkward enough.

"I'm comfortable sharing a chair, but if you aren't..." She let the sentence dangle.

Dan stammered, "No, I'm fine."

"OK, so you picked your client from the list, and now what?" She said.

"Then I select which disks need to go into the fantasy session. It's really more complicated than this, but I don't create the software. I just plug in the files." Dan was happy to have an audience.

His love for computer technology was a mania that ruled his days. He often lost all track of time when he was tinkering around on the computer, alone for days or even weeks, seeing no one but his clients. He stocked up on groceries for two weeks at a time, did his banking online and had no reason, other than work, to get out of the apartment. Even his love for the gym didn't get him out. During his "mania" days he used the fitness room in the apartment complex.

"That looks easy enough. So like if there's a character in the fantasy, it will be real to the client?" She looked at the "character disks", taking them out of their cases.

"Yeah, it will feel real, with the gloves and goggles on." Dan frowned. He didn't like her touching his stuff. He chided himself for being so childish. It was no big deal. *I need to get out more, stop being so neurotic*, he told himself.

"Wow, so if the client chooses a real life person to have a fantasy about, would the client believe in the fantasy after the session is over?"

"I doubt it." Dan said. He took the CDs from her hands and put them carefully back into their cases.

"Why not?" She didn't seem to mind that he had taken possession of the CDs.

"Well, we give the client a Memory Enhancing Shake, to boost the experience. It's a temporary thing, sort of like the effects of alcohol." Dan was finally growing weary of explaining all of this to her. He was initially pleased in her interest in his job, but now her inquiries were becoming tiresome.

"What if the client continued to drink the Shake on a regular basis, or drank large amounts?" She said, eyes aglow. "Would that make him believe in the fantasy after the session was over?"

Dan frowned. "I don't know, maybe the effects would last longer. I'm not sure. I don't think it's something we need to worry about."

"Sorry for asking all these questions, I was just curious." She said. She stood up from her perch on Dan's leg, which had painfully fallen asleep.

"I guess it could cause problems, but we are careful. Each shake is measured carefully in safe amounts. I can see what you mean though, there is certainly the potential for lingering effects." Dan said. He was relieved that she was out of his lap. He'd be even happier when she was out of his apartment.

"Interesting." She said. Her lips curled into a smile that was no where close to pretty.

Dan shuddered. Ms. Right she was NOT.

15

~~~Action Jack~~~

```
You work for the CIA.

You are on a covert mission involving
the FBI and a drug ring.
```

    Jack had been anticipating his fantasy session all week. He had the attention span of a rabbit and could hardly contain his energy. He trimmed the trees in the yard just to give himself something to do.
    Elizabeth had lost patience with his boyish excitement, especially after Jack brought some of the Memory Enhancing Shake mix home. Dan

warned him not to overdo it on the drink, but since a little extra helped build muscle tissue, *why not?* But it wasn't going over well with Elizabeth. She was paranoid that the drink contained some sort of controlled substance.

Jack cracked his knuckles, one finger at a time. He waited for the lights to dim. A few minutes later he heard the *click*. Jack blinked his eyes to adjust to the light changes.

There he was!
Virtual CIA agent Jack was in the driver's seat of a black sedan. He was roaring down a gnarled country road, in absolute blackness. Up ahead he could barely make out the faint red blur of tail lights, the car he was pursuing.

"Ahah!" thought Jack. "They are trying to shake me." Jack pressed his foot to the floor, causing Virtual Jack to do the same. The car lurched forward, closing the gap between the sedan and the Mustang. Even in the dark, Jack recognized the car to be a Mustang from its distinctive tail lights.

Jack was exhilarated. The chase was utterly thrilling! With no real life danger! *Yet with the sensation of the ride of a lifetime.* He was flying at 95 miles an hour, and climbing.

Suddenly the Mustang swerved. Jack jerked his body. Virtual Jack did too. The car was now keeping pace with the Mustang, side by side, on the country road that was becoming narrow.

Up ahead Jack could see a farm, with a pole barn ablaze with lights. There were several cars scattered on the land. He realized too late that *armed men* were outside these cars, waiting to greet him.

"What do I do now!" Jack shouted aloud. He had no idea what he should be doing! There were no rules to this thing!

Would you like to make a selection?

Jack nearly jumped out of his skin at the sound of the computerized voice. The remote control buttons were lit. Jack clicked a button.

Would you like to add characters to your session?

Jack clicked "Yes". He was given a menu of photos and options. Jack picked a large man with a boyish face to be his partner. He picked several more men to be his back up. He pressed "Enter".

Instantly a large man was seated next to Virtual Jack. Behind his sedan were five more cars in hot pursuit of the bad guys at the pole barn. *Cool*, thought Jack. Wish fulfillment. *Totally cool*. He now had a partner and plenty of back up.

Virtual Jack followed the Mustang onto the farm property. He stopped the car and threw open the car door. He saw his partner reach into his jacket for his gun, so Jack did the same. He held a cold hard gun in his right hand for the first time in his life. It was a feeling he didn't want to duplicate in real life.

Both men got out of the sedan. The men at the barn opened fire. Jack went into action.

The confrontation happened so quickly, Jack didn't have time to think about it. He shot and was shot at. He dove for the dirt, his skin hot with abrasions from sliding on the gravel.

When it was over, one of the agents was down. Most of the "bad guys" were down.

Only one man was left to chase, the driver of the Mustang. He was Virtual Jack's nemesis. That man would live for another day, another fantasy session.

The lights came up. Jack let his breath exhale slowly.

He was perspiring profusely. His hair was matted to his forehead, his hands were sore from clenching his fists. His skin was hot. What a rush!

16

~~~Vince and Sharon~~~

Vince envied his younger brother Jack's full head of blond hair. He himself was stuck with a bad comb-over of brown strings that always looked greasy. He really didn't mind that much, but he knew that Sharon was bothered by it. Why else would she insist that he wear a hat when they went out?

And the paunch. He knew it had become unsightly. The kids affectionately called it his "beer belly", but he winced each time they said it. He didn't *want* to be a sweats-wearing sloth, watching the game from his nasty old couch, eating pizza, drinking beer. But that is exactly what he had become, and he knew it.

Vince felt old. Old and broken down. He'd been born old, born without that spark that Jack had. The spark that Jack *still* had. Sharon was always quick to point out the differences between him and his brother.

Jack got two promotions in the past year, while Vince had not had a substantial raise in eight years. Jack worked in the creative field of advertising, while Vince had a "boring" job in sales. Jack was the kind of father who was "Daddy" to his kids, Vince was not, not even when the kids were little. He'd been plain old Dad from day one.

Jack and Elizabeth had a new family picture taken every year for their Christmas cards. The cards were sometimes handmade, sometimes purchased. They arrived each holiday season with the new photo and a cheery form letter that Elizabeth sent to all of their friends and family. *We are doing well, the kids are beautiful, our life is perfect, blah, blah, blah...*

Sharon didn't bother to send cards. She was too cheap to toss a few bucks at cards, too lazy to make them, and too bitter to wish anyone else a happy holiday.

She didn't *want* to get a family picture taken with her slob of a husband. Or with the kids. Who, she never voiced aloud, looked like they were standing in a police line up, thanks to Derek's tattoos and piercings and Casey's midnight blue hair.

Oh the list goes on. Really, though, Sharon would be happy if only Vince made more money. He knew she was miserable at her job. She hated being a hairdresser.

While it was fun to gossip with the customers

and the other hairstylists, many of whom really liked Sharon, she hated her new boss. A girl young enough to be her own daughter, it was infuriating to take orders from her. The girl wanted to shorten their smoke breaks, monitor how long they were out for lunch, and didn't let them fill in for each other.

Gone were the days of swapping dates with her friends when she wanted to go out. Now she was stuck with whatever schedule they gave her.

She wanted to quit work and stay home, as Elizabeth was doing. She resented that Elizabeth had the luxury and she didn't. It's not that Elizabeth and Jack had money, she knew they didn't. But Elizabeth was the type who didn't seem to mind. Sharon didn't want to live like that.

Sharon's kids were grown, or technically they were. So she wouldn't be staying home to raise children like Elizabeth was. She simply didn't want to work. She wanted to travel, she wanted to shop, she wanted to be pampered.

She had worked long enough. She wanted life to be about *her* for a change. She raised her two kids, and it wasn't easy with the lug of a husband she had. He'd changed maybe a dozen diapers total.

During the years when the kids were little, Vince was going to sales conferences and working nights so often that he really wasn't around much. Sharon may as well been a single mother. Of course she didn't work in those days, but still, it wasn't easy.

Today she was *done* doing the family thing. She wanted to start having fun. Sharon's resentment grew stronger every day that passed without Vince getting a promotion. There wasn't much fun without money.

Vince also felt the gap between him and Jack widen. He would never have what Jack had, and he despised him for it. He couldn't bear seeing Jack hold his daughters, laughing with his sweet and pretty wife.

But Vince let his bitterness go, just like everything else in his life. He turned his thoughts back to the game, and popped open another can of beer.

17

~~~Michelle~~~

Michelle slid the 8 x 10 glossy photo on the flatbed scanner until it was lined up with the edge. She admired her own image when it appeared on the computer monitor. The long blond hair, the full sensual lips, the long slender legs. She could have been a model. Maybe she still could.

She selected a file format to save the picture, saving the file to a disk. She slid the disk into her open purse and punched a few numbers into the phone. "It's Michelle," she said.

"Where are you calling from?"

"Work."

"What? You twit!"

"Relax! No one's here but me."

"Did you get it done?"

"Yeah, no problem. Hey, can I keep the photo?"

The question was ignored. "Did you send it?"

"I put it on disk. I thought sending it over the Internet would be too risky, too easy to trace that."

"You're right, good idea."

"So that's why I'm calling. Who do I give the disk to?"

"Drop it by my place."

"OK. Tonight?"

"I'll be here."

"OK then, I better get off the phone before anyone shows up." Michelle put the phone down. She was satisfied to be the one to hang up first.

She hated the mind games they played with her. She was glad to have that little errand over with. She glanced at the clock. She had just enough time to grab some breakfast before everyone else came to work.

18

~~~Fantasy Session 2~~~

Dan's greeting was lacking it's usual vigor. The muscle man looked smaller in the vertically striped dress shirt he was wearing. No purple tee-shirt today.

"Anything wrong?" asked Jack.

"My apartment was ransacked last night. I was out late, went to the movies with Stacie, the woman I was telling you about. When I got home, I found a big mess."

"Oh man! Did they take anything?" Jack said, genuinely concerned. He knew where Dan lived. He was startled to hear that someone had broken into his place. His apartment was in a good area.

"No, just messed things up. But they got into

my paperwork and files, so I was up all night trying to get today's Virtual sessions organized. I don't understand it. Who would break into my apartment just to throw stuff around?" Dan was obviously shaken.

"Old girlfriend jealous of the new one?" Jack tried to come up with an explanation. It didn't make sense to him either, breaking in just to mess up the paperwork?

"No. My last girlfriend was Lisa, and she lives across the country now. Besides, we split on good terms." Dan shook his head, clearly baffled.

"Wow. I don't understand it either. I'm glad they didn't take anything. Maybe they didn't find what they were looking for, jewelry maybe."

"I had cash sitting out in the open, it was untouched. Why didn't they at least take the money?"

"I don't know, Dan. Did you call the police?"

"Yeah. They sent someone out and I filed a report. But since nothing was taken, no one's going to waste their time with it."

"Maybe someone thinks you're a spy," Jack took a stab at humor to lighten the situation.

Dan smiled and clapped his hands. "Well enough of this, you've got a session! Action again, I see."

"Oh yeah, I've got to catch that guy in the Mustang!" Jack wore the eager grin of a ten year old boy in an amusement park.

"Jack Miller?"

"Yeah?" Jack stood up. His headset was already strapped, so it was difficult to stand. He was startled to hear a sudden voice in the room.

"I have your shake." The man's voice was hard and low. He unfastened the straps, removing Jack's headset and goggles apparatus. His face was pitted with old acne scars and his eyes had the look of a dim-witted thug.

"But I already had my shake." What was this all about? Jack shook his head in confusion.

"You're Jack Miller, right?" The man held the drink out toward Jack. His gnarled arm boasted an unusual tattoo, of a Siamese cat.

Jack accepted it. "Yeah."

"They told me to bring this to you." The man turned around to leave. He paused at the door, looking back at Jack. His face looked vaguely familiar. Jack assumed he'd seen him around Virtual Memories before.

"Dan didn't say anything about that." Jack said slowly. He still held the drink.

"Dan sent me in here. He forgot to give it to you." The man said casually. He seemed disinterested in Jack, impatient to leave the room.

"OK, thanks." Jack sat back down. He noticed the man was lingering, probably waiting to see if he would drink the shake. Jack drank it, eager to get rid of him.

"Have a nice trip, Jack." The man called as he left the room.

The lights were dimming, the session was already starting. *Have a nice trip?* What was *that* supposed to mean? Jack grabbed the headset, quickly forgetting the vague unsettling feeling he had. All he wanted to do was play the game.

Abruptly Jack was swept away, barreling

down a dark country road in a sedan. The same sedan as in his earlier session. He squinted his eyes. Yes, the same faint glow of the Mustang's tail lights.

Why was he getting the same scenario as before? Dan had described a setting in a foreign country, Russia maybe. So why was he back on the country road?

Jack could see a pole barn coming up ahead. It *was* the same session! Had there been a mistake?

Dan said that his files had been a mess after the vandalism on his apartment last night. Could that be it?

He wondered if he should take off the goggles and walk out, find Dan. He didn't want to pay for the same session twice. But when he tugged at the straps, he discovered that he couldn't get them off without some help. *Oh well, it was no big deal to do the session again.*

He was alone in the car. Should he select a partner and back up as he had done before? No, he wouldn't bother. He'd see what would happen if he let Virtual Jack drive up to the pole barn alone.

As he neared the pole barn, he could see the driver of the Mustang. He was out of the car and standing under a beam of light. A short man, about 5 and a half feet maybe. Red hair, athletic build.

He looked like a man who could have been in the military. He probably didn't need a weapon. He looked like one of those "human weapon" types. Karate, special forces stuff.

Jack changed his mind about letting Virtual Jack handle this alone. But when Jack reached for the remote control to select back up characters, he realized that he didn't *have* the remote. His heart raced. Where *was* it? Why wasn't the keypad lit up so that he could see it?

He couldn't find it in the deep blackness that surrounded him. He could see only the faint glow of the dashboard and the yellow beams over the pole barn that was fast approaching.

Jack felt himself stop breathing, as if he were having a nightmare. His body was stiff. He felt unable to move. *He was terrified.*

He was incapable of leaving the room. He'd never find the way out of the blackness even if he *could* get the headset off. He had no choice but to hope that Virtual Jack would survive without the virtual backup team. He sure didn't want to watch himself die, virtually or otherwise.

SCHEEE!

Jack grabbed the headset with both hands, rocking back and forth in sheer agony. The noise stopped and the visual went dark. Nothing.

Jack sat in the dark purple silence, stunned. What happened? When would the lights come up?

Vrup!

The visual was back up, sound too. It was the pole barn again, but this time he heard music.

The driver of the Mustang was gone.

Virtual Jack was alone, standing in front of the barn. It sounded like a party was going on in there.

Jack could do nothing, having no remote control to make selections. He could only experience what Virtual Jack was doing. He hated the lack of control, it was like having a nightmare he couldn't wake up from. He had no choice but hope he would wake up soon.

Virtual Jack walked into the pole barn, and went in. There was a woman in there. Wearing tight jeans and no top. Jack tried not to stare at the woman's breasts. He forced his eyes up to her face, a face that looked familiar to him.

Michelle! he thought, shocked.

"What is going on?" the real Jack said aloud. Michelle didn't work at Virtual Memories. How did she get on the character file?

But the Virtual Jack said nothing. He walked steadily toward the blond woman, who was now beckoning him to come closer.

The real Jack shrank back into the leather chair, pushing his body away from the image before him.

Virtual Jack did not respond to his movements. He grabbed Michelle and held her body to his own.

"Hey, *DAN!*" Jack shouted. *"DAN!"*

He wanted no part of this. His heart was true to Elizabeth and the girls. He never once thought of straying. The very idea repulsed him. Jack longed for Elizabeth's sweet face to appear, begged for the session to end, tried to block the sensations from reaching his body. He closed his eyes, but there was no escaping it.

Michelle's hot breath was upon him. He smelled hairspray in her hair, and expensive perfume on her skin. He felt her full lips wet against his chest.

She wriggled and pressed her body ever closer to his, tearing at Virtual Jack's clothes. Virtual Jack did not try to stop her.

~~~ ~~~

The lights came up fifteen minutes later. Jack was disgusted with the dampness of his pants. It was a reflex he seemed powerless to control. Mortified, he slipped out the door, down the hall, and out the employee exit before Dan could see him in this sorry state.

Once in the parking lot, he quickly got into his car without being seen. He started the engine immediately and headed for home.

He felt disoriented and he had a headache. His skin smelled like old lipstick and perfume, and Michelle's womanly scent. He gagged, feeling that he would retch.

Jack stopped the car to vomit in a grassy ditch. The acrid smell clung to him. His nose and throat burned. He wanted to go home. This was all a bad dream. Elizabeth had been right, this wasn't something to mess with.

"*I'm so sorry, Elizabeth,*" he whispered, alone in his car. "*I'm so so sorry.*"

He broke down, hugging the steering wheel and crying. *"Dear sweet honey."* He cried for his wife. He cried for his girls. He wanted to go home.

~~~ ~~~

The traffic buzzed by the car, shaking it slightly. Jack picked his head up. His head pounded. He felt faint, weak. He didn't remember where he was. He was hungry.

He didn't remember where he was going. Slowly his mind seemed to grasp his situation.

Oh yes, he had been tailing the Mustang. He must have dozed off or something. Why didn't he know where he was?

Jack could see the man's face in his mind. Red hair, military build. He drove slowly back down the highway, searching for him.

He found the Mustang, in the employee lot of a business called Virtual Memories. Jack parked the car in the neighboring lot. He hated surveillance. It was the most tedious part of working for the CIA. Boring.

He dug in the glove box for something to entertain himself with while he waited. He found a kids' coloring book. Baffled, he tossed it on the empty passenger's seat. What was that doing in there, he had no kids.

About twenty minutes later Jack caught movement out of the corner of his eye. A man with red hair was coming out of the building. It was him.

Time to go, he thought. Jack let the man merge into traffic before he slowly followed him. He stayed three cars back. It looked like the makings of a long night.

19

~~~Following Jack~~~

"So why I am following him?" Karyn scrunched her nose. "I'm not sure I can do this."

"Oh it's easy. People don't expect to be followed. It's not like how the movies show it, where you have to hang back and drive through alleys. As long as you don't ride his bumper, he won't suspect anything." Serena chewed thoughtfully on her pen. "Well, unless he's paranoid or something."

"Swell. So I should hang back?"

"Just don't follow too close, but there's no need to get crazy with it. You're not the type to follow someone. He won't suspect you."

"OK." Karyn said grudgingly. She wiped the palms of her hands on her jeans. "So, I guess I should go find him, huh?"

"Yeah, go ahead. You've got your cell phone. Call me when you know where he is."

"Why am I doing this again?" Karyn fished in her purse for her car keys.

"Because we think there's something going on here. I suspect there's another client in the making and we might as well get started."

"Do you always start working before you get hired?" Karyn laughed. It was hard to stay angry with Serena. Besides, Karyn said she was game for anything.

"No, I usually don't. But I didn't like that Michelle woman. I want to be ready to help our next client. I just know there'll be one."

"And they'll come to you?"

"Yeah. Something tells me they will."

"OK, I got it. I'm not doubting your intuition, I'm just stalling. I don't like to drive."

"You don't? I'll follow Jack if you want." Serena shrugged.

"No, no, I can do it. It's, it's just that driving makes me nervous. I have to pump myself up for it."

Serena raised her eyebrows, but didn't mock her friend. "Take one of these." She threw a peppermint at her.

"A piece of candy?" Karyn caught the candy before it hit her in the face.

"I read somewhere that sucking on hard candy relieves stress. I always keep some around, it was always good to have during college finals."

Karyn laughed. "OK, thanks. I'll give it a try. Well, I'm off. I'll call you when I find out what he's up to."

~~~ ~~~

Karyn found Jack easy enough. He was sitting in his car near Virtual Memories. It was the first place she checked, knowing that he was a regular player there.

That's odd, she thought. He was in the next parking lot over. *What was he doing?* She probably wouldn't have noticed him there if there had been more cars in the lot.

Karyn parked the car where she hoped he wouldn't see her. She was grateful that she'd stopped at the Burger King drive through. She ate her sandwich while she waited for Jack to do something. She sipped her large Diet Pepsi.

Fifteen minutes later she was still sitting in her car, watching Jack sitting in his car. Except now her bladder was so full she could barely stand it. And she had a headache, maybe from the full bladder, maybe from the tension or maybe just because she had rotten luck sometimes.

Why didn't she have any Tylenol with her? She kept telling herself to put some in her purse, but...

Finally she detected movement from inside Jack's car. The dome light came on. She could see Jack's eyes riveted toward the Virtual Memories lot. *He must be watching the car pulling out of there,* she thought.

Then the dome light went off and his headlights flipped on. Karyn's heart raced. Yes, he was following that sports car. Jack pulled out the neighboring lot as Karyn started her own car.

This is really bizarre, what is he up to? Karyn allowed three cars to come between she and Jack. *That should be enough space to remain inconspicuous.* She hoped so anyway.

Karyn continued to follow Jack, who was following the sports car. *Who was the guy in the other car and why is Jack following him?*

Oops, Serena!

She'd forgotten to call her. At the next stop light she punched in the number.

Serena picked up right away. "Wilcox Detective Agency."

"Serena, it's me." The light changed and Karyn cradled the phone with her neck. She always kept both hands on the wheel in the 10 and 2 position she learned over a decade ago in her high school driver's education class.

"Where are you?"

"I don't know." Karyn said with surprise and panic.

"Are you lost?" Serena's voice revealed nothing, but Karyn guessed that she was amused.

"Well, I'm following Jack. And Jack seems to be following a guy in a sports car. I don't know where we are going or why. He was waiting for the guy to leave Virtual Memories and now he's tailing him."

"This story gets stranger by the minute. Stay on him, see what he does."

"I have to anyway. I don't know how to get

back home." Karyn laughed, but her voice was shrill even to her own ears.

"Oh don't worry, we'll be able to figure out where you are. Tell me what you see."

"Uh, a Blockbuster Video."

"Next to a McDonald's?"

"No."

"Next to a strip mall?"

"Yes!"

"OK, is there a gas station at the next light?"

"I'm at the light now, and yes, there's a gas station."

"Yeah, I know where you are. You're only three miles from this office, Karyn."

Karyn flushed crimson. "Well, I told you I don't like to drive." Flustered, she nearly cut off a minivan.

"Are you sure you don't want me to do this? I can be in my car and meet you on the road. I'm sure I can catch up to you in ten minutes or so."

"OK. Yeah, can you do that?" Karyn tried to still her voice, but she could tell it was shaky.

"On my way. I'm actually in my car already, headed toward you." Serena said. She balanced a slice of leftover pizza on a paper towel on her right thigh. Why leave it behind and let it go to waste? Her car often smelled like the inside of a pizzeria.

"What? How could that be?" Karyn sputtered. She looked around, almost expecting to see her.

Serena laughed. "You dialed my cell phone number. I got in my car while we were talking."

"Oh! So do you need me to tell you where I am now?"

"Yeah, are you at the bridge?"

"Yes, just about. Jack's there now, he's turning..."

"Right?"

"Yeah."

"OK, I'll be there."

"OK." Karyn gritted her teeth, waiting for traffic to allow her to turn. She hated driving. She eased into the turn and searched for Jack's car. *Whew!* She found him easily.

"I see the Mustang," Serena said triumphantly.

"The Mustang?" Karyn asked, confused.

"The 'sports car'. I'm guessing that you are talking bout the Mustang."

"Oh."

"It's the only sports car ahead of Jack." Serena said. "Yeah, it's the Mustang."

"Cool! Great! So you are on the other side?"

"The other side? Yes, I am in the opposite lane."

"Coming toward me?"

"Yes, Karyn, in fact I see you now." Serena grinned and waved. Karyn glanced at her briefly but did not take her hands off the wheel. Her neck was killing her from keeping the phone on her shoulder.

"Now you are going the wrong way, so what do I do?"

"Look in your rearview." Serena flashed her lights. "See, it's me!"

"How did you get there so fast?"

"I did a U-turn."

"In *this* traffic?"

"Karyn, there's nobody around. Behind me,

there's nobody. In fact, if we don't get more company Jack's going to notice us eventually."

"Then what do we do?"

"I think we should stay on him."

"OK." Karyn said, disappointed. As much as she wanted to know what Jack was doing, she just couldn't talk herself out of her driving phobia.

"I can't see Jack, is he turning off?" Serena asked, her voice muffled by a mouthful of pizza.

"Yeah, he's off, turned right. Why can't I hear you that well?" Karyn said. She didn't want to lose her connection to Serena. She knew she couldn't find her way back home.

"He's sure leading us out of civilization, isn't he? My cell phone must be getting fuzzy. Maybe my battery is dying." Serena said, shoveling the last bite of pizza into her mouth.

"Hey, you're eating something, aren't you?" Karyn giggled, a nervous titter.

"OK, OK. But it's gone now." Serena grumbled, caught.

"But how can you be on the phone, driving *and* eating pizza all at the same time?"

"I use my knees when I grab the pizza."

"*What?* Are you nuts? Your knees on the steering wheel?" Karyn was amazed and appalled.

"I only do it for a second, don't worry." Serena laughed.

"He's slowing down!"

"OK, stay calm."

"He's stopped! What do I do?" Karyn was nearly screaming. They had been driving for over twenty minutes. The darkness was thick around her. She had no idea where they were, some rural area. She had the creeps.

"Pull over to the shoulder and turn off your lights. You're far enough back, I don't think he's noticed you. I'm doing the same thing, right behind you."

Karyn pulled over. Whew! This was a nightmare. She was shaking. "Your phone is getting so staticky I can barely hear you."

"Can you see Jack?"

"Yeah. He's sitting in the car. He's watching the guy in the Mustang go into the second house, the one with all the lights on."

"OK, I'm right behind you. We'll watch him. See what he does." Serena said. Her phone really was starting to break up now. It wouldn't be much use soon.

"OK. But I really wish I could go to the bathroom."

"Ah, the joys of surveillance. This is where the boys have it a little easier." Serena joked.

"Jack's getting out of the car, going up the driveway to the house. He's—oh! He's got a gun! I see him under the lights, he's got a gun!"

Serena was a blur past Karyn's window. She ran flat out down the country road while Karyn sat frozen. Serena tackled Jack, taking him completely by surprise and sending him to the ground. The gun skittered down the steep driveway.

Karyn, now out of her car, ran toward the gun. Jack was staring at the petite woman who had sent him to his knees. His face was blank, confused. Karyn picked up the gun, holding it far away from her, pointing it toward the ground.

"Don't move." Serena called out. She rushed

toward Karyn and retrieved the gun. "I'd feel better if I had that."

"So would I." Karyn said weakly. Her body trembled and her throat was a ball of cotton. She couldn't find the strength to swallow.

Jack simply said, "Where am I?"

The door to the house opened and the driver of the Mustang appeared. "What's going on? Can I help you people?"

"I hope so. May we come in?" Serena took Jack by the arm and led him to the house.

Startled by the sound of an approaching car, the group whirled around to face the dark road. The car slowed, then pulled into the driveway. A muscular man stepped out of the car. Even in the darkness his face was easy to recognize.

"Dan?" said Jack in a strangled voice.

"Curiouser and curiouser," whistled Serena.

"You're the private detective, right?" Dan bounded over to where the group remained huddled under the porch lights.

"Yes, I'm Serena Wilcox. This is my associate Karyn, and you are Dan, from Virtual Memories. I spoke with you earlier when I was making some inquiries about Jack."

"Yes." Dan smiled. "You didn't ask me anything that I couldn't tell you."

Everyone looked first at Dan. When it became apparent that he wasn't going to keep talking, they turned their attention to Serena. The driver of the Mustang was the first to break the silence.

"Come in. It's cold out here." They followed Bill inside. He gestured toward the livingroom furniture and then sat down on a high backed rocker.

Serena, Karyn and Dan took the overstuffed hunter green sofa. The sofa was so new that the factory sticker had not yet been removed from it. Each of them felt a twinge of guilt for using it.

Jack sat in the second rocker, a matching high backed style. His hands lay in his lap, his shoulders loose. His eyes were fuzzy with disorientation.

"I'm Bill. Bill Rogers. I work at Virtual Memories, so I already know Dan." Bill said gently. His words seem loud in the room. The only competing noise was the metallic ticking of a large-faced decorator clock that hung on the wall above the sofa.

"So, Jack was following Bill. And Karyn was following Jack, who was following Bill. And I was following Karyn, who was following Jack, who was following Bill." Serena laughed.

Dan nodded. All eyes were on him. He cleared his throat. "I was following all of you."

Serena laughed. Karyn joined her. Soon everyone but Jack was laughing uproariously. Jack didn't sway from his limp stupor. Their laughter seemed to confuse him even more.

"But why were you following us?" asked Karyn. She was becoming impatient with everyone. She was heart weary from her brush with the gun, she was physically exhausted and she had to pee.

"I was looking for Jack, and I found him in the other lot, sitting in his car. Then I noticed that she," Dan jerked a thumb in Karyn's direction, "was sitting in her car. When she didn't budge until Jack started to move, about ten or fifteen minutes later, I figured she was tailing him. I followed behind Karyn. Then at the bridge, I saw Serena fly by, waving. Then she did a U turn, nearly cut me off-"

"What? I didn't see anyone behind Karyn!" blurted Serena.

"Obviously." Dan grinned.

"Oops, sorry."

It was the first time Karyn had seen Serena blush. Maybe it was the pain from the full bladder talking, but she was naughtily delighted to see Serena squirm.

"No harm done. Anyway, I followed all of you here, to Bill's house. But I got stopped at the 4 way stop, which no one else stopped for, and was too late to stop Jack from pulling the gun. Glad you got him."

"What gun?" Bill leaned forward, alert.

"Jack was going to kill you." Dan said simply.

"What!" yelped Bill, Serena and Karyn in unison. Jack said nothing.

"Bill?" For the first time, the group noticed a young blonde woman standing in the adjoining kitchen. Her eyes were filled with fear.

"This is my wife Jennifer." Bill said, in an inappropriately cordial tone, as if he were introducing his wife to colleagues at a company party.

Jennifer smiled weakly and walked over to where Bill was sitting. She looked at him questioningly. A private look was exchanged, but the *What is going on?* question was written all over her face.

A baby's sudden and jarring cry made everyone jump. "Oh, the baby's awake..." Jennifer's eyes darted from Bill to the source of the urgent sound. Clearly she didn't know which way to turn.

Bill squeezed his wife's arm. "It's OK. Go get Hannah."

Jack lifted his head. "I have a Hannah too."

Then he dropped his shoulders again and his eyes glazed over.

The others looked expectantly at Dan, and when he didn't say anything Serena yelped, "Tell us what is going on!"

Dan continued his story in his own mellow way. "I figured out that my girlfriend was conning me. I'd stopped by Jack's office to see why he left his session..."

"Back up, you're losing me." Serena frowned.

"Today Jack had a fantasy session. It's where we program a story, like a movie, and the client feels like he's a part of that story. Jack had a session today, but he left before it was over. I was concerned so I went to his office to see if he was there." Dan paused.

When no one spoke, he continued, "When I got there, I noticed my girlfriend's car in the lot. I thought that was strange, since I didn't think they knew each other. Well, I went in, and I saw her from across the floor. And I saw her desktop. It said her name was Michelle. That's not who she told me she was."

"Ah. I know this Michelle. She hired us to find out what Jack was doing at Virtual Memories. But how were you convinced that this was her desk, and that she'd lied to you?" Serena's eyes gleamed with interest. This was starting to go somewhere. In the cobwebs of her mind the pieces were coming together.

"She saw me. And she screamed." Dan laughed. "It was pretty obvious that she thought I'd caught her. But I really hadn't. I'd been looking for Jack, not her."

"Caught her at what?" Serena interrupted.

"She said 'You can't prove anything. I'm not gonna talk to you, so why don't you just leave.'"

The group stared at Dan, mesmerized.

"Then what happened?" Karyn prodded. It was excruciating the way he took his sweet time telling the story.

"Then I left. I had no idea what she was talking about. I knew she'd lied to me about who she was. And that she worked for Jack. It wasn't a heartbreak for me, I wasn't planning on seeing her again anyway." Dan said.

Karyn picked up on that little piece of information. This hunk was single, single, single. He was worth having a full bladder for. Cute smile too. *I must be crazy to be thinking like this now*, she thought.

"*And?*" Serena had to resist the urge to reach over and strangle the man.

"Well, Jack mysteriously disappeared after his session. I kinda put two and two together, since she was asking me so many questions about how to program fantasy sessions." Dan smiled, triumphant that he'd solved a mystery.

"What are you talking about?" Serena said. She controlled herself, trying not to let her impatience show. But his slow manner of getting to the point was making her crazy!

"I figured she must have tampered with Jack's session. She'd been asking me some questions about how the fantasy sessions worked, and she knew that I kept the files at my place. After my apartment was vandalized I slowly put two and two together." Dan tried his triumphant smile again.

129

"But why would she want to do that, and what would it do? I'm not following you." Serena said.

Bill creaked forward in the rocker. "I think I know where he's going with this. You think that she changed his fantasy session, that she deliberately did this to Jack."

"Oh I *know* she did it. After I left Michelle, I followed up on my suspicions." Dan said. He stopped talking

When he saw that Serena was so impatient that she looked like she was about to lunge at him, he continued, "I took a look at Jack's session file. She'd messed with it alright. She wrote herself in as his love interest."

"Ooh!" Karyn and Serena breathed together. Karyn said, "But why did Jack go after Bill with a gun?"

"Bill was on the character file, as the bad guy in Jack's fantasy. Something went wrong. Jack must still believe he's in the session, working for the CIA." Dan studied Jack's expressionless face. "I think he's had too much of the ME."

"ME?" Serena asked. This man was giving her the story in fragmented bits. It was killing her!

Bill stood up. "Memory Enhancing Shake. It's a chemical drink we give clients to enhance the experience." He stretched his legs. "There really hasn't been much testing done on it, but it's safe in the small doses we give out. We don't know what happens if they drink larger quantities."

"*What?* How can you be in business with a potentially dangerous and untested drug?" Serena said.

"When I joined Virtual they showed me

documentation of testing. I wouldn't give a client something dangerous." Dan said. His face was red with anger and embarrassment.

"Hey, that's just what I've heard. After this, I'm sure someone will be investigating them." Bill shrugged. "Who knows if we will have a job when this is all said and done."

Light was peeking behind the curtains. It was dawn. Everyone had eaten, used the bathroom and had a couple of hours to rest. Their conversation had stretched beyond Bill's patience.

"I appreciate you all trying to get to the bottom of this, but can I ask you to take this to a coffee shop so I can catch a couple of hours of sleep before the kids get up? I don't think *this* guy's gonna kill me." Bill stared bleary-eyed at Jack. Jack was dead asleep, sitting straight up in the rocking chair.

"Yeah, of course. Thanks for the sandwiches and everything." Dan extended his hand toward Bill.

"I'm sorry we kept you up all night, crashing in on you uninvited." Serena said sweetly. "We'll be taking everything to the police when we have our act together."

"Hey, you saved my life. I owe you." Bill gave her a quick hug. "OK, now get. And take the big lug with you." As if on cue, Jack opened his eyes, stood up, and obediently followed the group out the door.

20

~~~Helen~~~

Elizabeth dreaded the visits to the nursing home, especially since Helen had been moved to the hospital building. But she never missed a visit. Her beloved mother-in-law's health had been steadily failing for months, and for the past three weeks her condition was critical. It was unlikely that she would ever recover.

It was excruciating watching such a beautiful person go through this much agony. Elizabeth silently wished that the woman she so admired would pass peacefully in the night. It was an unjust world that would allow this magnificent human being to suffer a slow and horrible death.

"Liz." Helen clasped Elizabeth's hand. "I'm so glad you could come. How are the girls?"

"Keeping me hopping as usual. How are you doing today?" Elizabeth choked back tears. The skeleton of a woman before her was not the vibrant powerhouse of a lady she had loved and admired from the day they first met.

"Lizzy, I'm at peace. Please don't look at me with those eyes. The nurses are keeping me comfortable and I'm not afraid to meet my maker." Helen smiled sweetly, her cheeks sunken with disease.

Just last year she'd been riding horses and swimming the lake. Now, fourteen years after her husband's death, breast cancer was taking her life.

What was the rhyme and reason for this fate? Why had cancer struck this family twice over? It was the age old question: Why do bad things happen to good people?

These spiritual questions nagged Elizabeth, depressed her. She sometimes lay awake at night and thought about spirituality, dark brooding thoughts that left her with more questions than answers.

What if faith in God was meaningless? What was the meaning of life? What if all events were random?

It was as if Helen could feel the weight of Elizabeth's troubled spirit, for she knew exactly what to say. "Liz, I want you to listen to me," she began.

Elizabeth nodded. She stroked the tight dry skin of the fragile hand she held. She grasped every precious word, to hold in her memory always.

"I believe that there is a will of God, and that it is my time to go. I am not afraid. I am ready to leave the pain of my physical body." Helen said in a steady voice. Her gray eyes were tranquil, like the water in a slow moving river on a lazy summer afternoon.

"But how do you *know* this? How can it be the will of God to let you suffer? And why would He want you to go, when so many of us love you so?" Elizabeth stumbled over those last words. A tear spilled over and trickled down her cheek.

Helen smoothed the salty tear from Elizabeth's cheek with her own warm hand. "There is a time for every event under the Heavens. It's my time. We don't question our time to be born. If we can accept our hour of birth, how can we *not* accept our hour of death?"

"But the pain? How can that be part of a divine plan?" Elizabeth hugged her own chest as if to protect herself from the sorrow she was feeling for Helen, and for herself.

Helen's voice was as gentle as the coo of a dove. "When we come into the world we bring tremendous physical pain to our mothers, followed by boundless joy. I believe leaving this earth is the same process, pain followed by boundless joy."

"I don't know how to have faith like you do. What if the people who believe in nothing, nothing more than a cosmic energy, are right?" Elizabeth's tears fell faster now. She pressed a tissue to her face. She had never discussed spirituality with Helen before, but time had a way of standing still when a life was in the balance.

Shredding the tissue with anxious hands, she continued spilling her fears, lifting the flood gates from within. "What if faith is just personality, just positive thought? Maybe religion is man's way of coping with life. How can you know for sure that it's not just something we *want* to believe?"

"Liz, not long ago your Hannah was a newborn baby at the breast. From the moment of her birth she was secure in your arms. She cried in fear when the nurse held her, or when she was alone in the bassinet. She *knew* her mother. How can we explain how she knew you?" Helen said gently. "She found comfort in you, peace. She had absolute faith that you would care for her."

"Some would say that's a biological instinct." Elizabeth said in a quiet voice. She didn't mean to argue, she was fighting hard to understand. She *wanted* to believe in something greater than herself.

"We can talk about science and evolutionary theories. We can study genes, cells, matter. But what's missing is the 'why'. *Why would matter work together to create, for no divine purpose, no higher plan?* Without purpose, there truly would be no point to living," Helen said gravely.

She whispered so softly that Elizabeth had to strain her ears to hear, "In a world that was not created by Love, there would be no hope. Grief would consume people. There would be no lasting inner peace. We could each create our own reality, our own morality, for none of it would matter."

"Yes. I see what you are saying. But how do you know? *How can you be so sure that there's a God?*" Elizabeth said.

Her porcelain face was like that of a china doll's, beautiful and delicate. Her eyes, framed by long dark lashes, were wide open, as if they were searching for the answers she so desperately sought.

"Liz, I can't convince you that there is a God.

Faith is a fuzzy concept to describe. I have faith in God the same way that I know how to read. Sometime long ago I learned to read, but I remember little of the experience. Yet I have enjoyed reading, I've learned from reading, I've found friendship and comfort from reading." Helen paused to drink water from a straw. The effort pained her, but her facial expression did not reveal it.

"This is how it is with my relationship with God. My faith is a part of me, the best part. It's how I can forgive others even when I don't want to. It's how I can feel blessed even when my life is not going well. It's how I can see the good in things."

"Oh Helen, I do see what you are saying. Your faith comes naturally to you. Why can't I feel that?" Elizabeth said, wanting to have a reason to believe.

"You have to be open to angels, to miracles and to God. Accept the good things that you know to be true. Don't second guess your own knowledge." Helen said. "Love God faithfully, and you will have faith in God." She coughed fiercely, doubling over. Her lungs seared with pain. This time her pain showed on her face.

Elizabeth willed her hands to stop shaking. She picked up Mrs. Miller's floral bound Bible. "Would you like me to read from Psalms?" Helen's favorite passage was bookmarked with a gold rope.

"Yes, dear, please do." Jack's mom closed her eyes and let her head sink into the hospital pillow. She smiled faintly.

21

~~~Serena Wilcox Detective Agency~~~

Jack hadn't come home the night before. Elizabeth was flooded with relief when she walked into Serena's office and saw her husband standing there plain as day. She bolted to him, clutching him around the neck.

He was slow to respond to her, but then grabbed her waist and pulled her to him. He whispered from deep in his throat, "I'm so sorry, I'm so sorry." He held her hair, brushed his lips across her forehead. He was scaring Elizabeth, who had never seen Jack act this way, especially in a room full of people.

Elizabeth broke from the embrace and met the eyes of the other people in the room. Seemingly in one breath, she said, "I am here to hire someone to find Jack, but here he is." She sounded both baffled and flustered. "Jack didn't show up to visit his mother yesterday, and he never came home last night."

"Where are the girls?" asked Jack.

"Mom came up to stay with them. Jack, I need to know what is going on! I called the hospitals, looking for you. Where were you Jack?" Her voice turned from wild desperation to that dreaded mix of spousal worry and anger.

Serena led Elizabeth to the only vacant chair. "I'm Serena Wilcox. I've been watching Jack, after we realized that something odd was going on."

Elizabeth's eyebrows furrowed. She studied Jack's face for insight into what was going on. She could not read his expression.

Dan extended his hand toward her. With a firm handshake, he said, "I'm Dan, from Virtual Memories. I'm sorry to say that we discovered that someone had implanted files into your husband's session, causing him some trauma."

"What? Why would someone do that?" Elizabeth's eyes were round with mounting alarm. Her palms felt itchy. She wasn't able to fully understand what they were saying, but whatever it was, it didn't sound good.

"That's what we've been up all night trying to figure out. I'm Karyn." She smiled kindly at Elizabeth. "This is George, a lawyer. We think we can help you get to the bottom of this."

"Thank you." Elizabeth said with the meek demeanor of a shy kindergartner on the first day of school.

"Jack's been pretty much out of it all night. I really should have called you, Mrs. Miller. I'm sorry that I didn't think of doing it." Dan frowned, disappointed with his lack of consideration for Jack's wife. He regretted encouraging Jack to play the Virtual add-ons. He felt responsible for messing up this guy's family.

"You have a strong case against Virtual Memories, and they have deep pockets. I took the liberty of having Jack checked out by a doctor, to document his physical and mental state. I can't see this thing even going to court. They'll settle quickly." George said with an authoritative baritone.

"I hope you don't mind that I called George Bowmann in, he's one of the best." Serena flushed, realizing that George seemed flattered by her compliments.

"Is Jack going to be OK? What happened to him?" Elizabeth's voice had dropped to a barely audible level. "And why are we talking with a lawyer?"

Her soft lashes were damp with the tears that she was fighting back. Elizabeth wasn't the type who cried easily. Tears shed over Helen, tears shed over Jack. She was on an emotional tightrope these days. Not herself at all.

"He seems to be coming out of it. The doctor thought he'd suffer no lasting effects." Karyn put her arm around Elizabeth, patting her shoulder. "He'll be just fine after some sleep."

"What exactly happened to Jack? What did they do to him?" Elizabeth asked, for anyone to answer. Jack looked like he had forgotten where he was. Feeling a sudden chill, she steeled herself for the news, whatever that may be.

"A woman he works with, Michelle..." Dan began. He noticed that Elizabeth flinched when she recognized the name. "She added a file to Jack's session, making herself Jack's lover in the fantasy." Dan cleared his throat nervously.

Elizabeth looked at Jack, who would not meet her eyes. Her face was flushed with humiliation and anxiety. "Did you have an affair with her?" Her voice sounded to her ears as if it were coming from somebody else. The seconds were an eternity.

"Not in real life, no." Jack whispered. "I'm sorry, Elizabeth, I'd never want to hurt you."

"I don't understand." Elizabeth's battle with the tears was lost. Wet streaks ran across her cheeks, dripping off her jawbone. This was undoubtedly one of the worst days of her life. The marriage she cherished was in jeopardy, revealed to her in a room full of people she had never met before.

"Jack didn't do anything wrong, but the session was upsetting to him. He had no control over what he was experiencing, and the ME shake he had was a larger dose than we'd ever give a client. He actually believed the fantasy was real." Dan paused. "He wasn't trying to hurt you."

"You wanted to be with this woman?" Elizabeth swallowed hard. "Michelle."

"No," said Jack. "I don't want anyone but you. Please believe me." He reached out to hold her, but when she recoiled from his touch, he settled for holding her hand.

"Michelle's plans didn't work. You don't have to worry about Jack being unfaithful." Karyn said. She hated seeing this woman so hurt, so raw. She felt guilty for being a witness to such private pain.

"I don't really understand what's going on. What's wrong with Jack? What is the trouble if no harm has been done?" Elizabeth pressed. She was having a hard time knowing what she was supposed to be upset about.

"The part of the fantasy that Jack continued to believed in, long after the session ended, was that he was in the CIA and was supposed to kill somebody." Serena said.

Elizabeth gasped, "What did you do?" She stood up from the chair and literally backed away from the group.

All of her senses were on overdrive. Her eyes were dry and raw from too many tears shed. The scent of Dan's cologne burned her nostrils.

"He didn't kill anybody." Serena said simply. "But he did pull a gun on a man named Bill Rogers. Bill works for Virtual Memories and was unlucky enough to be part of Jack's fantasy session that day. We stopped him before anything happened."

Karyn, who'd been standing close to Elizabeth until she left her chair continued, "We'd been following him, to see what he was going to do. Michelle had hired us originally, to follow Jack. She claimed she was his wife, which Serena found to be untrue. So we kept on watching him, even after we'd delivered the information she wanted."

"What? You were helping her hurt Jack and our family?" Elizabeth said with bewilderment, not anger. "Where did you get a gun, Jack?"

All that could be heard in the room was the gurgling of the coffee maker as the group thought about this new piece of information. Serena was the first to speak. "Jack doesn't own a gun?" She was kicking herself for not thinking of asking Jack about the gun.

"No. We don't believe in having a gun in the house." Elizabeth said.

"Where *did* you get the gun, Jack?" Serena asked. She couldn't believe she hadn't considered the idea that the gun might not belong to him. *Bad, bad, bad detective.*

"I was sitting in my car. The man gave it to me, told me I might need it." Jack slurred. "I was sitting in my car. He said I might need it."

"What man? Who gave you the gun, Jack?" Serena's face was a few inches away from Jack's, trying to keep him focused on the question.

"The man who gave me the Shake. I told him I already had it but he told me Dan sent him in. He told me to have a nice trip." Jack said, his blue eyes rolling back into his eyelids. He wouldn't be awake much longer.

Dan gestured for Serena to move out of the way. When she stepped back, he planted his feet directly in front of Jack and grabbed him by both shoulders. Looking him square in the face and lifting Jack slightly, he said, "Who was this man, Jack? What did he look like?"

Jack struggled to stay awake. "Scars on his face."

"Scars? Knife scars?" Dan asked.

"No, pits," he said.

"Acne scars?" Serena guessed.

"Yes." He said. "Ahh-knee sc-scars. Tattoo."

"Acne scars and a tattoo? What did the tattoo look like? Where was it?" Serena pressed.

144

"A c-c-cat."

"A *cat*?" Serena raised her eyebrows. She tried again. "Jack, what does the tattoo look like?"

"A cat. On his arm. A c-cat. S-simey cat." Jack's eyes were slits in his head, barely open, hardly focusing anymore.

"A Siamese cat?" Serena asked.

Jack didn't try to talk, but put his finger on his nose. Charades, "on the nose". Serena tried one last question. "Had you ever seen this man before?"

Jack mumbled something that sounded like he had seen the man before, but no one was sure. It would be touch and go until he was able to snap out of the stupor he was in. Probably not until after he had some sleep. Elizabeth watched him with round worried eyes.

George sat on the desk near Elizabeth, crossing his shiny dress shoes across pleated suit pants. He was impeccably dressed and professional. He considered himself to be the voice of reason, as did most people who knew him.

"The agency was hired by Michelle to look into Jack's activities. Surveillance on a spouse is the kind of work they routinely do, it often reaches my ears in a divorce case. Serena was doing you a favor by checking into Michelle's story and by continuing to look after Jack after she was no longer hired to do so." George said.

Serena basked in the glow of George's defense of her. She would remind him of it later.

"Thank you." Elizabeth said, humbled. The details still felt foggy to her, but she was beginning to get a feeling for what had happened. "Why would Michelle want to do this? Is she in love with Jack?"

Jack looked up, startled. "I don't think so."

All eyes were on Jack, who was slipping in and out of sleep. His moments of sudden clarity were unpredictable. Serena asked him directly. "So why would she do it?"

George grinned mischievously and addressed Serena, "Aren't *you* the one who should know the answer to that?"

Elizabeth turned to Serena, "Do we need to hire you?" Her eyebrows furrowed again, with obvious worry about the cost of hiring a detective. She had no idea how expensive it would be.

"How about you pay me from the money George will get for you? It's a sure thing that you will be compensated for this. I'll be able to cover my expenses upfront. OK?" Serena opened her hand in a gesture of goodwill.

"Thank you. We need your help." Elizabeth looked at Jack, who had fallen asleep sitting upright in the chair. She was grateful to have such capable people helping her. "I don't understand the whole CIA thing? And why aren't the police involved in this?"

Dan tried to explain. "It was a story, the fantasy adventure Jack chose as the theme for his session."

"Yes, I remember, but I don't see what the CIA and guns would have to do with Michelle," said Elizabeth.

"I don't know either." Serena said. "When Jack snaps out of this, let's go pay her a visit. Not all of us need to go, but I'll take Jack to see her."

"I'll go with you." George said, surprising Serena.

"OK, that's fine." Serena said, shrugging in an exaggerated show of nonchalance. "And don't worry, we'll turn everything over to the police. I just like to finish my job before giving it to them."

~~~ ~~~

"Yep she's here, I can't believe it!" Jack snorted angrily through his nose. He bounded the distance between the parking lot and his office without any awareness that he was clenching his hands into fists.

"Whoa, slow down. Why don't you sit in the car?" George held Jack's shoulders firmly. His suggestion was not a request, but an order. The two men stood outside the office door while Serena went inside.

Michelle recognized the petite brunette instantly. "I have nothing to say to you," she said huskily. She made a juicy smacking sound with her spearmint gum.

"Why did you plant the files in Jack's session?" Serena leaned into Michelle's desk, mentally taking a snapshot of everything. Her navy pants suit snagged on the metal edge. With a careful tug, she freed herself from the desk.

"I don't have to tell you anything, and there's

nothing to prove it." Michelle said with ignorant bravado. She pursued her haughty lips and tossed her brassy blond mane.

Serena's eye caught the scanner equipment near Michelle's computer and she took a gamble with her hunch. "We can prove it. You used the scanner to copy your picture file into Jack's session program. Even if you think you deleted everything, a sharp computer hack can trace everything you did. Nothing is ever really deleted."

Serena knew a bit about computers. She wasn't the 'sharp hack' who could actually find what they needed, but it was a good bet that Dan was. If nothing else, her bluff might get the confession she wanted.

Bingo! Serena thought smugly when Michelle's jaw dropped, the wad of gum dangling awkwardly at the edge of her bottom lip.

Michelle recovered quickly though, and snapped, "Get out of here!"

"Tell me why you did this. Are you in love with Jack?" Serena asked, doubtful the woman would tell her much. *Mostly* she was asking the question as an objective investigator working on a case. But part of her was thirsty for a juicy story, intrigued by the seedy details.

"Ha!" Michelle chortled. "Jack?" She continued to snicker as she tossed her lipstick stained gum into the trash can. She opened another stick and popped it into her mouth.

Serena lifted an eyebrow. "So why'd you do it? And what are you doing back here?"

"I work here." Michelle sneered. "I have no reason to quit my job."

"If you're not in love with Jack, why would you plant those files?" Serena tried to sound intimidating.

Michelle laughed with a shrill bark that could shatter crystal. "You aren't getting *'Jack'* from me!" Michelle obviously thought her pun was clever. She cackled even more, holding her sides as she laughed.

Serena rolled her eyes, trying not to let Michelle bait her.

George Bowmann suddenly loomed over the two women. "I don't find your humor charming or delightful. This case is going to court. It would be in your best interest to cooperate with us."

Neither woman had heard George come in, but his presence didn't startle them. One minute, he was just *there*, and Serena was grateful for his presence.

Michelle's lips curled into a grotesque snarl. "I don't care about Jack. He can have his little wife and kiddies. I did it for the money."

Serena and George hid their astonishment. "Who paid you to do this," asked Serena.

"I don't know." Michelle said bitterly. She was telling the truth.

"How did this play out? Why did someone hire you?" Serena continued.

"I got an envelope in my desk one day last month. It had my name on it, and it was sealed. It was a card that said to call the number."

"So you called some unknown person just because you got a card telling you to call?" Serena said incredulously.

Michelle shrugged. "Why not? I wondered what it was all about. Some woman answered and asked me how I felt about my boss Jack Miller. I told her that he was basically a putz. He thinks he's perfect with his little perfect wife and little perfect kids."

Serena tugged at George's sleeve. Jack had entered the building. George grabbed him and shoved him back out. He hissed, "Don't blow this!"

Jack left without a fight. George nodded at Michelle, "So you don't like him."

"I didn't say that." She tossed her hair with her practiced bob of the head. Then she came out from behind her desk. She hopped onto the front of it, making the computer monitor quiver.

"A 'putz' is what you called him," Serena reminded her.

"So? It doesn't mean that I hate the guy." Michelle said coyly.

"But you feel no loyalty toward him," Serena supplied.

"Right. Anyway, so then she asked me if I'd be willing to play a little trick on Jack..."

"She?" Serena asked.

"A woman, I don't know who. Anyway for $5,000. Yeah, I was willing." Michelle grinned. "I woulda done it for 50 bucks. It was easy. All I had to do was hire you to see what he was doing at Virtual Memories. I had to see if he was still going there, and when his next appointment was, who had him as a client. She didn't want me to do it myself. Said that it might tip Jack off."

"Why didn't this woman hire me herself? Why work through you?" asked Serena.

"I don't know, I didn't ask. Maybe she wanted it harder to trace back to her." Michelle blew small air bubbles inside the sugarless gum, then popped them with her molars. *Snap, snap, snap.*

"So you followed Dan and seduced him to get to the files." Serena hurried Michelle along.

"Yeah, that part was fun. Too bad he won't see me again." Michelle cackled. "I don't think he liked me much."

"Did you tamper with the ME shake?" George asked.

"The what?" Michelle's face was blank.

"The chemical drink they gave Jack before his session." George said impatiently.

"Oh, that. Yeah I think so. It wasn't me though, they paid someone else to do that part."

"How do you know this?" asked Serena. "And how did we get from 'a woman' to 'they'?"

Michelle smacked her gum. "*She* said 'they', you know. I think anyway, I got the impression it was more than just her. And I know about the drink thing because she asked me to do it, but then she called it off and said that I'd done enough. She said she'd get someone else for that."

"OK, so who is she and why did she want you to do this?" Serena asked, knowing she wouldn't get an answer.

"I don't know anything else. I called her at that number, then after Jack's Virtuous Memory game they paid me."

"*Virtual* Memories." George corrected, irritated. He was fed up with this woman. "How did they pay you?"

"They left the money in a post office box. $5,000 in cash. It's already spent, so don't even think about it." Michelle swung her legs, thumping her heels on the side of the desk.

"Give us the number." George avoided looking at the woman, whose lycra skirt was revealing more than he cared to see.

"If you want it," she scoffed. "I already looked into that. It's the number of a pizza place, it won't help you." Michelle lifted her short little nose into the air, like a haughty child.

George turned to Serena, "Pizza place? It might help Serena."

When Michelle was looking the other way Serena stuck her tongue out at George, a gesture that never lost it's power of expression.

Serena lowered her voice to the pitch of a purring kitten, "What do you know about the CIA fantasy and the gun?"

Michelle finally looked a little shaken. "I don't know anything about guns. No one told me about that. All I had to do is find out about the sessions, and get my photo on file. Someone else put the photo in. I don't know how to do that stuff. I don't know anything about guns."

"OK, we'll be in touch. I wouldn't leave town if I were you." Serena loved saying that old line. She hoped that she had shaken Michelle's confidence. The woman's arrogance got on her nerves.

Outside the office George said, "I bet this is just some rich guy's idea of a practical joke."

Serena shook her head, "No, I don't think so. I think this goes deeper than that."

"Deeper? What would anyone have on a guy like Jack? This sounds like an elaborate prank to me. Setting him up with a beautiful woman, trying to shake Jack up with the whole CIA game getting too real." George opened the door to his car, with the touch of his sleek remote.

"What about the gun."

"Was the gun loaded?"

Serena blinked. It was a question that she didn't think of. "I don't know. I dropped the gun off with the police. They are giving me a little more time to dig around before they get involved. They are tracing the gun for me though."

"I'll bet the gun wasn't loaded. I can't believe you didn't check. You're really slipping these days."

"You really think this is *just a joke*? That's incredible. I don't buy it for a minute." Serena let the insult pass, it was warranted. She *was* slipping these days. Maybe she needed a vacation.

"A joke that got out of hand. Someone just wanted to do a 'bachelor party' kind of prank on him, that's what I think. Doesn't Jack have any friends with money, who might do something extreme for kicks?" George said.

"Do you have friends like that?"

"No."

"Then what makes you think Jack would have friends like that?" Serena said. She was annoyed that he was making her case seem so trivial. A juvenile prank! "I bet you're wrong."

"OK, I'll take that bet." George grinned.

"Sure, I'm up for it. What's the prize?" She stared at him, her eyes shining. She loved a good game.

"Loser takes the winner out for dinner."

"OK, but I warn you, I don't eat light. I might look small, but I'll surprise you."

22

~~~Jack's back~~~

"I am so sorry, Liz." Jack said with a deep husky voice that made his wife feel cherished. Sometimes when Elizabeth called Jack at the office, she basked in the sound of his voice over the phone. His voice was in her ear now, recreating the chemistry of their newlywed years.

Jack massaged her tender shoulders. He stroked the silky skin under the collar of her flannel nightshirt, sweeping her perfumed hair off the back of her neck. His full lips brushed her exposed neck. She shivered.

"I know you are." Elizabeth whispered. She leaned into Jack's touch, letting herself relax. "I never really doubted you, but I was scared."

"I should have listened to you when you said something wasn't right. I'm sorry for being a jerk and spending so much money." Jack's jaw clenched.

"Why would Michelle do something like that to you, to us?" Elizabeth tried to keep her voice neutral, reflecting nothing but the security she had in their marriage, and her trust in her husband's faithfulness.

"I really don't know. Honey, you have to trust me, there's never been anything at all between us. I don't find her type attractive. I don't know why she'd do this."

"I know, Jack." Elizabeth said. "I trust you. It scared me at first, but I'm over that."

"When Serena and George confronted Michelle, she said that she did it for the money. I can't believe she'd sell me out so easily. I didn't know she had a problem with me." Jack peered into the darkness of the Miller's livingroom. He wanted to turn on the TV, but was aware that Elizabeth wanted to talk. He massaged her shoulders and waited for her to speak.

The Miller home was quiet and peaceful. Both girls were sleeping, cherubs in teddy bear blanket sleepers. Elizabeth was in a mellow mood. It was her wonderful "pre-Motherhood" self that Jack seldom saw during the stressful day-to-day life of parenting small children.

Elizabeth was baking oatmeal chocolate chip cookies, something she did when she needed to work off stress. The smell of the cookies was a warm embrace, a sweet comfort. Elizabeth was soft and beautiful. How could he have wanted to be anywhere else but here?

Jack studied the living room as if he had not been home in a long time. As always, clutter was strewn across the room. Toys, socks, this weeks' mail, even a crushed layer of graham crackers. Jack winced, hoping that the food wasn't ground into the carpet. *Let go of it*, he scolded himself. *It's not a big deal.*

He knew the children would be small for only a short time. He and Elizabeth would have many years ahead for living in a tidy home. When Jack would one day reach his senior years, he knew that he would gladly welcome dinosaurs on the floor, if only to hold his babies in his lap again. He knew this, and yet he had a hard time staying true to the important things in life. He vowed to try harder.

It was Jack who broke their quiet. "My obsession with those sessions almost made me lose you. I don't understand myself. I don't know how I could have gotten so caught up in the fantasy."

Elizabeth didn't know what to say, so she listened. She sat on the floor at his feet, leaning against his legs while Jack was sitting on the sofa.

"I really don't remember the past couple of days." Jack drank in the sweet smell of his wife, soap and skin, with a hint of the perfume he gave her last Christmas. "I think I was more upset about turning thirty than I thought. I don't know why, I guess because the girls demand our constant attention."

"Do you feel OK now?" Elizabeth's worry forehead returned.

Jack kissed it, right on the furrowed brows. "I'm fine. How are you?"

"I'm fine."

They looked at each other, saw the faces they fell in love with, young dreamers on the same lifepath. Elizabeth slid into Jack's lap and began to unbutton his shirt.
   A soft meowing sound gave them pause. They waited. The meow belted into a wail. Elizabeth sighed and left Jack to get Hannah.
   Jack watched his wife as she left the room. Elizabeth's steps were hurried as she raced to comfort the baby they loved. He didn't need a virtual reality. *This* was reality. And from now on, he wouldn't let it slip away.

23

~~~Dan~~~

Dan galloped out the door and across the Virtual Memories parking lot with the last box in his hands. He added it to the larger box already in the trunk of his car. That trunk held all the personal things that he'd had in his office, which really wasn't much. It was depressing to see how small his life was. It fit into two boxes.

He couldn't stay on at Virtual, now that he was aware of troublesome security issues, ethical concerns and the possible health risks from drinking the ME Shakes. He had to break free of any association with Virtual Memories, leave the ship before it sinks.

How something he was so passionate about

could be so corrupt, he didn't know. It made his heart sick. He wanted to believe that they were a company who cared about people, who wanted to make a difference. What they were doing at Virtual was extraordinary. They were giving people their own Self, the power to return to their past, to heal themselves.

Virtual Memories was not about money to Dan. And for the short time he had worked there, he honestly believed that the company was about more than the bottom line. He never would have suspected corruption or a health threat to his clients. Was there *nothing* in this world that was as good as it seemed?

Dan dreaded telling his family that he was leaving his plush job. But it wasn't as hard as he thought it would be. Having the golden career didn't make his relationships with family members any better, it just got them off his back for a while. The job gave his family something to brag about. But it didn't make them any friendlier toward him. Not sincerely, anyway.

At that moment, Dan glanced at the line of cars beyond the parking lot. He did a double take when he saw Jack's car stopped at the light. Elizabeth and the kids were with him. Dan smiled at the sight of a blond toddler's head bobbing around, barely visible in the back seat.

Who paid Michelle to set Jack up? Why would someone want to ruin him? Why Jack?

His eyes passed over the line of traffic behind Jack. He blinked at what he saw. Was it a coincidence? It was hard to imagine running into *two* people he knew, seemingly at random

Dan jumped in his car and made a kiss-off smooch with his hand toward the Virtual Memories building. Then he merged into traffic, several cars behind Jack. It was time to tail Jack again. Whatever this mess was, Dan felt responsible for getting him into, and for getting him OUT of it.

24

~~~Wilcox Detective Agency~~~

"You're eating *again?*" Karyn laughed.

"Yeah, yeah. Want some?" Serena slid a basket of cold greasy fries across the desk. She put her shoes on, tying the laces in a double knot.

"What *is* that?" She pointed at the mysterious gray pile in the Styrofoam container. The smell alone was revolting.

"Gyros. There's plenty here, help yourself." Serena's mouth was full.

"I'll pass." Karyn's own lunch felt unsafe in her stomach. "Are you going somewhere?"

Serena grabbed her car keys. "Yep. Guess who called?"

"I don't know, Jack?"

Serena brushed her hands across the thighs

of her jeans. "Yeah, he called earlier but he was just asking if we'd found anything yet."

"So who are you talking about then?"

"Dan. He is following Jack even as we speak." Serena's eyes danced in merriment. She hopped out from behind her desk.

"What? What's going on now?" Karyn held her car keys in a death grip, hoping she wasn't going to be asked to drive this time. Of course she *could* say no.

"Oh, he quit Virtual Memories."

"He did? Wow. Good for him." Karyn smiled.

"Do you *like* Dan?" Serena mused. She jumped onto the sofa, quickly folding her legs like a pretzel.

"What? Oh I never thought about it."

"HA! You've *never*? Yeah, right!" Serena said mockingly. She scooped up a pen from the coffee table and began clicking it up and down, in a manner that Karyn found most annoying.

"No, I really haven't. But I will now!" Karyn grinned. "OK, now what's the deal with him following Jack? I think it's funny we all have cellular phones. Seems silly almost."

"Yeah, I guess. Anyway, when Dan was leaving Virtual Memories, he saw Jack at the light."

"So? Why would he want to follow him?"

"Dan *also* saw that guy Bill, the man with the Mustang from Virtual?"

"Oh?"

"Anyway, he saw Bill behind Jack and figured it was too bizarre that Bill just happened to be there. Especially since Bill should have been at work."

"Yeah, that's too much. So he's following Jack

to find out what's going on? Jack must have taken the day off, huh?"

"Yep for both, Elizabeth said that Jack is taking a couple of weeks off actually," said Serena from her yoga-like perch on the couch.

"I'm assuming that Dan will tell us what is going on?" Karyn asked.

"He's supposed to call us when he finds something. Last I heard, he was headed out of town. He thinks they might be going to visit Jack's mom."

"I'm surprised you didn't take off after them." Karyn said nervously.

"I was thinking about meeting them there. We're on the edge of town, we aren't that far from the hospital where his mother is. We'd probably beat them there actually."

Karyn thought about it. *What else did she have to do that day, why not?* Aloud she said, "OK, but no more guns. Right?"

"I can't imagine anything like that happening."

"And you can do the driving." Karyn shuddered just thinking about tailing Jack that night, not knowing where she was.

"Of course. If you drive, who knows what town we'd end up in."

"Hey! I let you into my private insecurities and look what you do to me!" Karyn yelped. She snatched her purse and followed Serena out. "Besides, weren't *you* the one who cut Dan off in traffic when you made that illegal U-turn? When 'no one' was around?"

"Yeah, yeah. I've been driving since I was fifteen and I haven't been in an accident yet."

"Well don't make today your first time." Karen sniffed.

165

25

~~~The Woman~~~

"I see them, they're already here. Dan's hunch was right. He should have *my* job." Serena pulled into the back of the hospital parking area. She recognized Jack's and Dan's cars, now empty. And Bill's Mustang was unmistakable, with the fuzzy dice hanging from the rearview mirror and the suction cup Garfield sign in the back window.

"Dan must have gone in with Jack." Karyn observed the obvious.

Serena nodded. "Yep, but there's Bill. Sitting there. Waiting."

"Can he see us?" Karyn flipped her head around in panic.

"No. He doesn't have a clue that we're here. And I doubt he thought much of Dan meeting Jack here."

"Wouldn't he think it was strange to see Dan pull in after Jack at the hospital?"

"He knows that Dan and Jack are friends, he probably thought Jack asked him to go." Serena added, "Don't worry, he doesn't know that we are watching him."

"OK, I'll try to relax." Karyn said, fearing that her novice anxiety might be driving Serena nuts.

Serena reached across Karyn to get to the glove box. She took a small pair of binoculars out of a pink vinyl case.

"Does that come with matching earrings?" teased Karyn.

"Nope. A matching purse."

"You're kidding! Too funny!"

"Hey, I *use* that purse!"

"I've never seen you carry a purse."

"But when I *do*..."

"Which is *never*."

"Well, but if I ever do, I'll use my pink one."

"Just a wild guess, it's the only purse you own?"

Serena laughed, "Yeah."

"Hey, what's going on now?" Karyn's voice rose. She was anxious to have a turn at the binoculars.

"Bill's getting a visitor to his car. A woman. She's getting into the passenger's seat." Serena let out a low whistle.

"What? What?" Karyn squealed.

"She's all over him!"

"Oh yeah, I see *that*. I don't need binoculars to see that."

"Close up it's even worse." Serena put the binoculars back in the pink case. She gave them to Karyn to put in the glove box.

Karen stole a quick look before putting the binoculars away. She gasped at the larger than life proof of Bill's infidelity. "My, oh my. Bill's married. With that baby. And his wife's so sweet looking. Jennifer was her name. Oh I hate this. This makes me sick. In broad daylight too!" She slumped in her seat.

"I know. I hate this part of the job. People suck."

Both women contemplated the wisdom of that statement, depressed. They tried not to watch the couple enjoying illicit moments in the Mustang. It was like gawking at the scene of an accident.

"So who is the woman?" asked Karyn.

"I don't know. And how she fits in? I don't know." Serena frowned. "There's got to be a connection to Jack in this somewhere. It's too great of a coincidence that Bill ended up in the same place as Jack. I don't have any bright ideas about how he fits in."

"But we'll find out, right?" Karyn searched Serena's face for a clue to what she was thinking.

"Yep." Serena's eyes sparkled. "Guess what we're going to do?"

"Follow the girl." Karyn groaned.

"Good thinking." Serena folded her arms and slouched into a comfortable position. From the looks of it, it could be a while before the woman was ready to leave.

26

~~~Solving the Puzzle~~~

"Thanks for meeting us here." Serena said cordially. She slid into the red vinyl booth. "I hope you like Mexican food."

"I love Mexican food, thanks." Jack gestured for Elizabeth to squeeze past him into the booth opposite Serena. Then he sat down. Jack the gentleman.

Karyn sat next to Serena. "I love the food here, but I usually end up eating so many chips that I'm full before they bring the entrees out! So I end up having something to take home."

"This is my kind of restaurant. Food now, and food later." Serena grinned.

As if on cue, a young blonde waitress bounced

over to the table, waving a large basket of warm chips. She gave them a variety of salsas and took their drink order. She left four glossy full color menus.

Elizabeth patiently waited until their server left the table. "What did you want to talk to us about?"

Jack patted his wife's knee under the table. "They'll tell us, don't worry." His voice was low, his protective "husband" voice.

Serena smiled, "That's OK, I know you guys must be anxious. Let's decide what we want to eat and then I'll fill you two in on what's going on."

It seemed like an eternity before the perky waitress returned to the table, pen in hand. Jack ordered something spicy that he'd never tried before. Serena ordered the taco platter. Karyn and Elizabeth both wanted the sampler plate.

"OK, so now we get started." Karyn said. She glared at Serena, who was munching on a tortilla chip.

Serena took a quick sip of her diet soda, then she began. "How much do you know about your sister in law?"

"Mine?" said Jack.

"Yes. Sharon Miller, married to your brother Vince." Serena said flatly.

"Oh I don't know. She's a bit of a shrew. She and Vince have been married a long time. Their kids are older. I don't know, like what?" Jack was bewildered. He exchanged a look with Elizabeth, who was not as surprised as Jack appeared to be at where this was going.

"Would it surprise you to learn that she's

having an affair?" Serena stole another tortilla. She avoided looking at Karyn, who was sure to chastise her lack of social skills.

Jack's mouth gaped open. "Wow, yeah, it would."

Elizabeth laughed, "Oh it doesn't surprise me at all. Jack's just not very good at reading people. Sharon's been unhappy with Vince for years. I'm not surprised, not surprised at all."

"Oh?" Serena's eyebrow shot up.

"I'm just surprised that she stays married to him." Elizabeth took a sip of her soda.

"Interesting." Serena said simply.

There was a collective pause, while the group munched on the chips, each lost in thought. Karyn was the first to speak, "So what we were hoping to find out, is what possible connection this has to your case."

Jack shook his head. "How can these things be related? So my sister in law screws around, how does that affect me?"

The waitress arrived with the steaming plates of saucy food. She cautioned them that the plates were hot. After seeing that the group was impatient for her to leave, she bobbed her head in a cheerleader fashion and left them alone.

Karyn began, "It relates to you somehow. The man she's seeing is your virtual nemesis, that guy in the Mustang."

"Whoa! You've got to be joking, she's sleeping with *Bill*?" Now she had Jack's interest.

"Is it possible that Sharon could have had something to do with tampering with your session?" Serena asked, feeling them out.

"But why would she want to do that? Why set Jack up and not Vince? What does having an affair have to do with Jack?" Elizabeth was skeptical.

"We don't know. But there's got to be *something* to this. It's far too great of a coincidence that she's having an affair with Bill, the *same* Bill that was in your virtual session." Karyn said. She was beginning to understand Serena's excitement. The bug had caught her, too.

"I see what you are saying, but I just can't come up with any reason why Sharon would want to tamper with..." Elizabeth stopped talking in mid-sentence, her fork frozen, her eyes were saucers.

"*What?*" said the group in unison. All three of them were leaning in toward Elizabeth. Breathlessly awaiting her response.

"Would you care for any..." sang the bubbly waitress.

"NOT NOW!" All four of them snapped.

Blushing furiously, the waitress spun away from their table, tossing the bill on the table as she left, even though it was obvious that they weren't finished with their meals. It was doubtful she would come back. Serena regretted not asking for a refill of soda earlier.

Elizabeth began, "You know, Jack's mom is very sick. Terminal actually."

"Oh, Liz, what are you *thinking?*" Jack moaned.

"Oh I think I know. Is there a substantial inheritance involved?" Serena was quick to make that leap.

"Yes, there is. And there's a will. Everyone

knows about it. I mean, everyone in the family knows." Elizabeth glanced at Jack.

"Am I missing something, did anyone mention that Jack's mother is wealthy?" Karyn frowned.

"I just took a guess. Money is a big motive for all kinds of outrageous things. Go on," urged Serena.

Elizabeth continued, "Well, there's Jack, his sister Pamela and his brother Vince. All three are married, with kids. Jack's mom is very family oriented. She's written her will so that Jack, Pamela and Vince all get 500,000. If they are married (and all are) they each get an additional 500,000. That's supposed to be divided among any children they may have (they all have kids). *If there's a divorce, they don't get that second amount.* The second 500,000 will be divided between the other two intact families."

Serena mused, "So if Sharon leaves Vince, then Vince's share is half a mil, not the full million."

Jack said, "Right. And she'd have to fight to get her share of the $500,000. So if she stays with him, she could get her hands on a million dollars."

"So why didn't you two tell me this before?" Serena threw up her hands. "A million dollars! That's enough motive for a million different crimes! A no brainer!"

Jack shrugged apologetically. "I didn't think about the money. I guess I'm in denial about Mom, I keep hoping she will pull through this. I don't like to think about her will." Jack's voice had become deep and gravelly. It was hard to make out what he was saying.

Elizabeth patted Jack's hand under the table. The group settled into a comfortable quiet, eating the last of their meals, and sipping their drinks. They mulled over the mystery at hand.

"I get why she doesn't leave Vince. But we still haven't answered the question about why she wanted to set me up." said Jack.

All three women looked at Jack as if he were a silly little boy. "Of *course* we have," said Karyn.

Elizabeth touched his arm. "If she broke *our* marriage up, then our 500,000 'family' inheritance gets split between Pamela and Vince. So she'd get even more money."

Karyn said simply. "So it's all about money."

"Greed," said Serena.

"Sex," said Jack.

"Just like a man, thinking of sex first," laughed Elizabeth.

"Which makes me wonder how Bill fits into all of this. How involved is he?" Serena thought aloud.

"And what about Vince?" asked Jack. "How much does my brother know."

"Jack? You really think he might be in with her on this?" gasped Elizabeth.

"I hope not," Jack replied glumly. "But it might be possible."

27

~~~Dan~~~

NEET NEET NEET!

Dan's alarm clock screeched at him from its perch on his oak dresser top. Dan slapped a beefy hand over the "snooze" button to silence it. Then he let himself sink back into his blissful slumber.

NEET NEET NEET!

NEET NEET NEET!

Dan shut the alarm off for good this time, and forced himself out of bed. He was meeting Bill at Virtual Memories, training him to take over Dan's position.

Bill is an odd duck, Dan thought. It was rumored that he was having an affair with one of his clients. Sheesh, what a sordid thing *that* was.

Bill's pretty young wife Jennifer seemed oblivious to her husband's philandering ways. What a shame. Dan flinched at the thought of that poor girl's heart breaking when she would inevitably one day uncover the truth.

And their baby girl, how could he do this to *her*? Dan despised men like Bill. *Men like him are why women learn to hate men*, he thought angrily.

Dan drove to the familiar brick Virtual Memories building, but did not see Bill's car. He was not surprised. Bill was notoriously late for things, while Dan was typically early, even after hitting the snooze a few times. Dan allowed himself what he called a "wake up buffer", a few extra minutes to hit the snooze button without making himself late.

Dan used his key to get into the building, a key he wouldn't have much longer. He waited in his office for Bill to show up. His office was barren of his personal belongings, but no one else had taken it over yet. So it still felt like Dan's office. He would miss this place.

"Hey, big guy." Bill swaggered into the tiny room.

"Whoa there, have you had a few too many Bill?" Dan was amazed. It was 7:00am on a Tuesday! Why was the man drunk?

"You might say that." Bill smirked. He stumbled toward a chair and slowly lowered himself into it. He still fell rather than sat, but it wasn't much of a drop.

"Can I ask why you are drunk at 7:00 in the morning?" Dan asked with genuine concern.

"The woman dumped me."

"What woman?" Dan asked. Maybe it was probably none of his business, but Bill *made* it his business when he showed up drunk on Dan's time.

"Sharon. Gone. She don't want me no more." Bill slobbered and spat as he ranted.

"Your *client* Sharon?" Dan tried to keep the contempt from creeping into his voice.

"Yeah, Jack's sis." Bill blathered. He belched a horrible acidic burp that Dan could smell.

"Jack's sister?" Dan said in disbelief.

"In-law. She dumped me. Got what she wanted and left."

"I should take you home. We won't get anything done with you in this state of mind." Dan sighed. He wondered if Jack knew that Sharon had been a client at Virtual Memories. Probably not, he guessed.

Bill continued to whine. "Shoulda seen through her. Was an idiot."

"Come on, Bill, let's get on your feet." Dan started to move toward Bill.

Bill's head wobbled and jerked forward. His eyelids closed longer with each blink. "I should'na done that to my Jennifer."

"No, you shouldn't have." Dan said flatly.

"I gonna go to sleep now." Bill's head dipped lower, his eyes shut. "I don't wanna talk about that woman no more."

"Bill, get yourself together. People will be here in about an hour. We have to get you somewhere else. Come on!" Dan shook Bill roughly, something he admitted to himself that he had no remorse in doing.

"I helped her. I helped her set Jack up." Bill confessed. Spittle dripped from the right corner of his ruby lips.

"*What?* Why would you do that? Why did she want you to do it?" Dan was flabbergasted. "What possible reason could you have?"

"Money, man. It's always about money. And sex, lotsa sex." Bill laughed with an eerie high pitched cackle. "Sharon gave me sex, I helped her set Jack up."

"And the money?" Dan knew he wouldn't be able to keep Bill alert much longer. He gave him a firm shake. "What about the money?"

"Uh huh." Bill slurred.

"The money? Come on, Bill, stay with me!"

"Yeah, she said someone was going to give her some money if she played a little joke on Jack. So I helped her."

"A joke?"

"Yeah, some practical joke she said. To get even."

"But why? Get even for what?"

"I dunno. I just did it. Thought she loved me. After I did it, she dumped me. She's gone. Gone, gone, gone." Bill tried to stand on his wobbly legs. "Gone, gone, gone."

"Let me give you a ride to..." Dan groaned. He couldn't take him home, he couldn't do that to Jennifer. He sighed. "OK, Bill you're coming home with me." He threw a muscular arm under Bill's short frame and dragged him like a rag doll to the parking lot.

28

~~~Karyn's session~~~

Karyn was the first one at the office. She chided herself for accepting the key that Serena had given her the day before. *Serena will have me opening up every day so she can sleep in until noon,* she grumbled.

The phone rang shortly after Karyn set her dripping umbrella on the vinyl floor mat. It was Dan.

"Hi there!" he sang.

"Hi." Karyn imagined Dan's dimpled grin. He was the happiest man she had ever met. "You never called us after you followed Jack to the hospital."

"Oh, yeah. I forgot. I didn't learn anything

new that day, but I did meet his mother, nice lady."

"It's sad that she's not doing well."

"I hope she passes peacefully soon. She's in a lot of pain." Dan's voice reflected a genuine respect for this human tragedy.

"I'm sorry to hear that she's in pain. That must be hard on the family."

"Yes. Especially in light of some new information."

"New information?"

"Yeah, I learned that Bill was having an affair with—"

"With Jack's sister-in-law, Sharon."

"Oh you already know?" Dan sounded disappointed. "So you know all about the set up."

"The set up? No! I sure don't. She had something to do with it? A member of Jack's own family?"

"Bill helped Sharon set Jack up. He doesn't know why she wanted to do it. He says she wanted to get even with a practical joke." Dan added, his voice full of sarcasm, "Some joke."

"No offense, but why is he confiding in you?" Karyn asked, trying to follow what he was saying.

"Sharon dumped him. He's drunk, or at least he was. He's sleeping it off at my place."

"I can't imagine that practical joke theory being true, can you?" Karyn scoffed.

"No, it doesn't make sense to me either."

"What goes on in that family? Too weird."

"I called you because I thought maybe you should come down to Virtual Memories, see if we can figure some stuff out."

"You've lost me. What would we find there?"

Karyn scrunched up her nose in concentration.

"Sharon used to be a client of ours. Maybe there's something in her file to help us figure how all of this comes together."

"Whoa! This thing is getting too strange."

"Yeah."

"Sure, I'll be there. I was hoping Serena would show up before we got off the phone, but she's probably still in bed if I know her."

"Do you want to wait for her?"

"Nah, I'll just leave her a note. Do you want me to come right now? Aren't people working now?"

"Yeah, that would be great. No, there aren't any sessions scheduled right now, there shouldn't be anyone there."

"OK, see you in a few minutes."

"OK."

There was an awkward silence, when neither knew how to end the call. Then Karyn said, "OK then, I'll let you go. See you there." She ended the call, then dialed Serena's number. No answer. Sheesh.

Karyn left her wet umbrella behind and ran to her car, throwing the hood of her jacket over her head. She was soaked by the time she was behind the steering wheel. The rain was coming down in sheets, exactly the kind of weather that she hated to drive in the most.

Fortunately the rain let up a great deal before she reached the end of the street. She was at the brick red Virtual Memories building in a few short minutes, minutes that Karyn spent with her knuckles white as she clutched the steering wheel in a death grip.

Dan was waiting for Karyn in the lobby. When she reached the door he noticed her pale coloring. "What's the matter, do you feel all right?"

Karyn blushed. "I'm just a nervous driver. I feel fine."

Dan smiled. "A lot of people don't like to drive."

Karyn was relieved he wasn't going to tease her about her driving phobia. "I don't drive very often. I just can't seem to shake my fears."

"Thank you for coming, especially since you had to drive in this weather."

Karyn blushed deeper. "No problem."

"I think we should try to get to the bottom of this right away."

"Oh yeah, I agree with you 100%."

Dan walked down the long corridor, with Karyn slopping along behind him, spraying the hall with water from her wet shoes.

"I hate to sound ignorant, but I really don't understand this Virtual Memories stuff," confessed Karyn.

Dan opened a door on the end of the corridor and gestured for Karyn to go in. It was like something out of a science fiction movie.

"This looks like the inside of a space ship," she gasped.

Dan laughed. "It's designed that way for effect. None of this is necessary. It's kind of hokey, I know."

"Oh. The lighting is all for show?"

"Pretty much. Any old light would have been fine. All we need is a chair and that headset. Oh, and the remote control, it's like a mouse for a home computer, to choose options. It operates like the remote control for a VCR, well sort of anyway."

"Wow. Pretty fancy games. Must be something. I can't imagine spending so much money on a game."

Dan grinned and raised an eyebrow. "I'll give you a session on the house."

"Can you do that? Didn't you quit working here?"

Dan laughed. "I cleared out my stuff and gave my two weeks notice. But officially I'm still an employee."

"OK, I'll do it." Karyn shrugged. She tried to appear nonchalant, an old childhood response to being challenged. She half expected Dan to goad her by saying, "You aren't chicken are ya!"

"Get into the chair. I'll get you a ME Shake and get your session ready."

"Wait a minute. What's the deal with the drink?"

"It's harmless, just enhances the experience."

"What about Jack?"

"You won't be having a fantasy session like he did, just a basic memory one. Besides, he was given too much of it. I really don't see any harm in having a small amount."

"Elizabeth said she'd had a strange reaction to the drink."

"Psychosomatic probably. If you really don't want to do this..."

There it was, the *chicken, chicken*, thought Karyn. "No, I'll do it. It's OK. Bring on the drink."

"OK, I'll be right back. Put on the headset, it will teach you how to use the remote control."

"OK." Karyn put the headset on. The straps hung loose. Having no idea how to fasten them, she let them hang. She squinted her eyes, trying to see something. Nothing happened.

"Oh, oops, I forgot to strap you in."

"*Strap me in?*" Karyn squeaked.

Dan bellowed with laughter. "I meant, that I need to adjust the headset so that it fits your head. You won't experience anything until the straps are in place."

"Oh." Karyn flinched. She was looking like a neurotic fool. *Calm down*, she told herself.

"There you go. All set now." Dan clicked the last snap. "And I brought your drink too, go ahead and drink it."

"But you just strapped me in. How can I drink it?" she said with surprise.

Dan stammered. "Oh. Yeah. I don't know how I could have..." He fumbled with the straps, letting her free. He was looking like a buffoon. *Get a grip*, he told himself. The back of his hand brush against Karyn's lips. Dan tried not to show any response.

Karyn drank the shake, as quickly as she could over the nervous knot in her throat. She couldn't understand why she was acting so uncontrollably goofy. She wasn't *that* intimidated by the session.

Dan hovered at her right shoulder, waiting to re-adjust the straps. When the headset was back in place, he jogged out the door.

"Hey! Where are you going!" Karyn yelped, but she was abruptly silenced by the wonder in front of her. The lights, the sound. She was floored. No wonder people spent so much money on this. This was incredible.

Karyn browsed through the menu, learning how to make selections. There was a momentary pause while Dan arranged for her session to begin. Karyn used the time to think about which day in her life she wanted to revisit.

She selected a date from her childhood, hoping to bask in her favorite memories with her cherished parents, who had died in an auto accident a few years ago. However, much to her dismay, the scene that came alive was confusing and disturbing.

The virtual experience was overwhelmingly real, in all of her senses. The smell of antiseptic invaded her every pore. A steady motor ground, ground, ground into her eardrums. Her vision was a bit hazy.

She looked down at her hands. They were so little! Child's hands, soft and smooth. Her feet wore blue sneakers. She'd written something on the inner soles of her shoes. What did that say? Karyn squinted her eyes, straining to see the letters. She chuckled, it read "I like boys".

Karyn knew this child was *herself*, and it felt so real. But why was the imagery so nightmarish? Where were the familiar objects of her childhood bedroom? What was the deal with the horrid antiseptic odor?

At that moment a man entered the room, a man dressed in white. A man with straight white teeth and a deep even tan. *Ugh, I don't believe it!* Karyn moaned aloud. Of all the random memories she could have hit upon, Karyn had relived going to the dentist.

She tried clicking the remote control, desperate to leave the dentist chair before drilling began. Unfortunately, the anesthetic was making her sluggish. She could barely move. *Oh no! I gotta get out of here!*

"Help! Help!" she shrieked. Her body was limp, she couldn't move a muscle. Soon, she knew, she wouldn't be able to stay awake.

The lights snapped on, the show over. Dan removed the headset as fast as his thick fingers could unsnap the straps. He held Karyn firmly by the shoulders and stared intensely into her eyes.

"Are you OK? What happened?" Dan grasped for breath, having just run full sprint down the corridor.

"I'm OK, I think. But I can't move my body." Karyn slurred.

Dan's eyes were large with alarm, "What do you mean? What happened?"

"I-I-I was..." Karyn's eyes began to close. "I..."

"You?" Dan shook her body gently.

"I was at the d-dentist."

"*HA HA HA HA!* Oh Karyn! The dentist! *HA HA HA HA HA!*" Dan doubled over, laughing until tears ran down his cheeks. He tried to regain his composure, but lost it again, laughing until he gave himself hiccups.

"Funny for *you*." Karyn snapped. Then she grinned. "OK, so it's funny. That's just my luck. Of all memories to go back to, I wind up at the dentist."

"*HA HA HA HA!* OK, OK, enough! I can't laugh anymore. My face hurts, I've got the hiccups." Dan grabbed his side, which had a stitch in it. "You're OK now?"

Karyn smiled, enjoying the warmth of Dan's laughter. "Yes, I'm fine now. That really *was* incredible. Maybe I'll try it again one day."

"Maybe with some careful planning, huh?" His eyes twinkled. "At least you got to see what it's like."

"Is that how a typical session is?" Karyn asked.

"Well, clients usually have an introductory session, that teaches them how to use the program. Then, yes, they have thirty minutes to do what you just did, unless it's a fantasy session, which is a whole different thing."

"Wow, thirty minutes is a long time," said Karyn, amazed. "As incredible as this is, I can't imagine becoming obsessed with it. And I don't think I want to mess with the fantasy stuff."

The two fell into companionable silence. They couldn't hear the clap of thunder outside the brick walls. All they could hear was the sound of air coming from the vents.

Dan left Karyn's side, saying, "So, now that we're through playing, want to follow me into my office? It's pretty bare in there, but I still have a computer connected to the network."

"Yes, of course." Karyn immediately got to her feet and shifted into a more professional tone of voice. She followed Dan to his small office. He was right, it looked bare.

"Wait, I'll get another chair." Dan found the adjoining office unlocked. He returned with a chair on wheels and rolled it up to the computer desk.

"What are we looking for?" said Karyn. She tried to imagine what Dan thought they could uncover.

"Well, Sharon was a client here. And she is the one who, I suppose I should say *allegedly*, set Jack up. I thought we might find some clues to her rhyme or reason from her files." Dan began punching code into the computer.

"You have her files?"

"No, not really. The network does. She wasn't my client, she was Lamont's."

Click, clickety, click.

Dan continued typing, but his eyebrows began to knot up. He frowned.

"What's the matter?" Karyn peered into the monitor. "What does that mean, 'No Match'?"

"I don't get it. It won't let me locate the file. Says it's not there. Maybe Lamont never uploaded it to the network."

"So we can't access it?"

"Lamont's office is unlocked, I could log on to his system."

Karyn gasped, "But isn't that illegal?"

Dan laughed, "No, her file isn't part of Lamont's private records, these records belong to the company. Everyone has a password though, so we'll have to try to guess what his might be."

"I don't know," said Karyn, shaking her head.

Dan rolled the two chairs back into Stewart Lamont's office. He booted up the computer and waited. The stench of cherry candy made his nose itch. Dan pushed Lamont's trademark bag of candy to the far edge of the desk.

"He's a strange man, isn't he?" Karyn observed.

All of Lamont's trinkets were lined up in a

tidy row on a long shelf covering the entire back wall. An apple paperweight, a book, a clown bank, a brass dog figurine. Over twenty or so objects, all lined up with about half an inch of space between each. Karyn imagined this man measuring each object so that every piece would be exactly the same distance apart.

"Yeah, he's a creepy dude." Dan clicked away on the keyboard, trying various passwords he could think of.

"Ooh!" Karyn drew in a sharp breath. "This is too weird."

"What is?"

"Don't you see it? The apple, the book, the clown? *ABC!* He lined all of his stuff up in alphabetical order." Karyn gestured toward the shelf behind Dan's head.

He spun around in the chair. "Yikes, that *is* strange. I never noticed that before. Something about that shelf was nagging at me, but I never could put my finger on what it was." Dan scowled. He would have been better off not knowing about this new oddity. He wasn't a fan of Lamont's to begin with.

"Do you think maybe his password is something like that? An alphabetical thing?"

"Maybe. Like maybe the first ten letters of the alphabet? The password can be up to ten characters long." Dan typed "ABCDEFGHIJ" and pressed "enter".

"It worked!" Karyn clapped her hands.

"Great, I'm in!" Dan said triumphantly. "I don't know how you figured that out, but thanks."

Dan reached the client file menu and typed

"Sharon Miller." The hourglass whirled briefly. The screen said "Cannot locate file. File has been moved."

"UGH!" Karyn yelled.

"No, this is nothing, I can get around this." Dan typed a command at the prompt. The screen said, "File found. Would you like to open file?"

Dan pressed "enter". The screen called up Sharon Miller's file. It was all there. Along with a bunch of stuff he wasn't expecting to see.

"Eew!" Dan blinked his eyes and hurriedly scrolled down to the bottom of the page, past the vivid color picture of a naked and unfit Stewart Lamont.

"GROSS! What's he doing with *that*?" Karyn pulled her chair in closer to the monitor.

BIZZ BIZZ

Karyn screamed, Dan jumped to his feet.

BIZZ BIZZ

"It's the door." Dan pressed the button on Lamont's desk. "Who is it?" he asked as steadily as he could manage.

"Serena Wilcox. Karyn said I should meet you here?" Serena's voice sounded very far away, but a most welcome sound.

"Yeah, come on in, we need your help." Dan buzzed her in.

29

~~~The Lamont Connection~~~

"Glad to see you finally crawled out of bed." Karyn smirked.

"I was awake, I just didn't want to go out in the rain. Figured if there was something going on, you'd call me." Serena pouted.

"I tried, you didn't answer."

"I must have been in the shower. Why didn't you leave a message on my answering machine?"

"Ah, well, I left you a note." Karyn shrugged.

"*In the office*! Anyway, that's why I didn't come right away. How long have you been waiting for me to get here?" Serena glanced from Karyn to Dan.

Dan ignored the question. "We found something interesting. I don't know what to make of it."

"OK, show me." Serena was at Dan's heels, bounding the corridor to Lamont's office. Her shirt was soaked.

"Why didn't you wear a coat?" Karyn asked.

"I didn't want to bother." Serena called over her shoulder. Karyn was dragging along behind them.

At least Serena didn't *smell* like wet dog. There was only the faint whiff of Pert shampoo from her stringy mop of wet hair.

"We have about an hour left before someone shows up. So we can't be in here long." Dan sat in front of the computer.

"Will that be enough time?" asked Serena.

"I think so." Dan scrolled back to Lamont's photo. There was no way a naked picture of him could look good.

Serena blanched. "That's not what I wanted to see on an empty stomach. Eew."

"So why would that be in Sharon's file? We don't get it." Karyn said.

Serena squirmed back and forth, shifting her weight from one foot to the other. It was her childhood habit of thinking something through.

Not more than a minute later, she tossed her head back and howled. "WhoEE! This is good."

Dan said, "What is? You figured it out already?"

"Sure. How do you think Sharon knew how to set Jack up? I bet that Lamont's been messing with her sessions, putting himself in *her* files. She knew how to do it, because her *own* sessions were tampered with." Serena said triumphantly, her face shining.

"Ugh, I bet you're right. What a pervert." Karyn said in disgust.

"Yeah, I'd buy that. I know Stewart. He *is* a pervert." Dan agreed.

"I wonder how much he knows." Serena said.

"What you're saying is that he had a thing for Sharon and messed with her sessions." Dan said. He grabbed a pencil and wrote four names on the top sheet of Lamont's neon memo pad: Michelle, Lamont, Sharon, Bill. He always thought better when he wrote things down.

"You can cross Michelle off from the list. She doesn't know anything beyond what we already know." Serena said while reading over Dan's shoulder.

"OK." He scribbled a line through her name.

"How did Bill get into this, beyond the affair? How do you know he was involved in tampering with Jack's session?" Serena asked.

"He told me. He was drunk, after Sharon dumped him." Dan picked up the phone. "In fact, he's still at my place sleeping it off. I'm going to call him and tell him to come here."

"Good idea." Serena said.

"Nah, there's no answer." He hung up the phone and continued to scroll through Sharon's file.

Again, something made him pause. He grabbed the memo pad and jotted down the numbers on the screen.

"What are you doing?" asked Karyn.

"What's that, some kind of code?" Serena peered over Dan's shoulder at the monitor.

"I'm not sure yet. I'll look into it and get back

to you. It looks like a corporate account, but I don't know why it's in her file." Dan muttered. He slipped the paper into his pocket.

"What are you doing now?" Serena asked. She hated not knowing what was going on.

Dan clicked away at the keyboard then said, "OK, here's the transcript of her sessions, the fantasy ones that she requested."

"She was a big player huh?" Serena whistled. Sharon must have dropped a nice chunk of change on these games. Maybe she got herself into a little financial trouble.

"Oh yeah. She probably spent more money than she has. Seemed addicted to the sessions. Then one day she stopped coming. Maybe the husband had enough." Dan scrolled down the transcript.

Karyn shouted. "Wait, wait, back up!"

"Where?" Dan and Serena said in unison.

Karyn touched the screen. "Look at that! She had a session about the money!"

"We got this woman cold!" Dan cheered.

The three of them read the transcript silently as fast as their eyes could skim through the words.

"Her fantasy is all about getting Jack's wife out of the way so that she can have her share of the inheritance. *Proof* that she wanted to set Jack up. What more do we need?" Karyn nudged Serena gleefully.

"Hmm. I think we should dig deeper. This is too easy." Serena said slowly.

"*What?* What more could there be?" said Karyn.

"That's the end of this file. I copied it onto a disk. We need to leave now, before someone shows up." Dan said.

"Too late. Knock, knock." Bill stood in the doorjam, smiling weakly at the trio. The three eyed him wearily, saying nothing.

Bill began, "Look, I know I've been an ass, cheating on Jennifer, and playing that joke on Jack. But I'd like to help you if I can."

"You could serve time for what you call a 'joke'." Dan warned. "Virtual Memories won't hesitate to press charges for messing with Jack's session."

"Yeah I know." Bill said sheepishly. "I thought if I were cooperative..."

"Oh puh-*leeze*!" Dan moaned. "No way!"

"Wait a minute, let's hear what he knows." Serena said.

"You can get me a deal?" Bill pleaded, looking at that moment like a true weasel, black shiny eyes and all.

"I can't make any promises, but I'll try." Serena said flatly.

Dan groaned in frustration. "This better be good."

"OK. So I know that Sharon was having an affair with Lamont." Bill noticed with dismay that the trio weren't impressed with that tidbit. "But I guess you already know about that, huh?"

Serena nodded. "We figured as much. He messed around with her session?"

Bill laughed. "Oh I don't know, he might have. But she owed him. She owed him money."

"*AH!* So *that's* it!" Serena snapped her fingers. "She was addicted to these sessions and borrowed money."

"Yeah, I guess. He was giving her lots of money, or something, cause I heard them talking one day. He said, 'remember you owe me' and she said, 'yeah, like you're ever going to leave me alone'."

"Wait a minute, so it might not have been about money." Serena waved a finger at him.

Bill shook his head. "I don't know what else she could have owed him."

"How do you know she was having an affair with Lamont?" Dan said.

Bill's face became red, the vein on his forehead prominent. "Because when she dumped me, she said that she didn't need my favors anymore, and that soon she would be able to stop screwing Lamont too."

"Oh! Well, that's that then." Karyn said, stunned.

"I can't believe I got involved with that tramp," Bill said bitterly.

"Do you know anything else?" Dan said.

"No. Just that Sharon owed Lamont and that soon she wouldn't have to owe him any more." Bill said nervously. "I can try to find out more for you."

"No, you stay out of it." Dan said.

"Bill, when did Sharon say that? About not owing Lamont much longer?" Serena said.

"It was just yesterday." Bill said. He glowered in memory of his moment of humiliation.

"Let's get out of here, before someone else shows up." Dan rose to leave. He put the chairs back in place and surveyed the area, making sure they left the office the same way they found it.

198

30

~~~Sharon~~~

Sharon slammed the door behind her. She was soaked. Her jeans were damp, her hair was dripping water onto the floor and the brown grocery bag she held was nearly falling apart.

The sky had burst open the very moment she left the store. The short jog across the parking lot to her car, without an umbrella or a coat, was a disaster.

She dropped the soggy grocery bag on the floor and kicked off her shoes. She heard Vince and her brother Martin in the kitchen. Swell, she thought. Never a moment alone.

"That you, Sharon?" Vince called. The starchy smell of pasta boiling drifted down the hall.

"Yes, I'm back." Sharon snipped. She knew she wasn't in one of her better moods, but she didn't care. Vince should know by now to stop breathing down her neck.

He is such a dolt, she thought. Vince didn't have a clue about what Sharon was scheming, or even that she was chronically unfaithful to him. *Loser.*

"Jason called. He's coming over after work." Vince said, unaware that Sharon was in another funk, a black mood that could last for days or even weeks.

"At least he's still got a job." Sharon said under her breath. Their son drifted in and out of their home. Sometimes he stayed with them, sometimes he crashed with a friend. He had his own place every few months but it never lasted very long.

"And Kathryn will be here, with Tom. So I thought we'd get a video or something." Vince said cheerfully.

"Whatever." Sharon didn't like her daughter's boyfriend. She didn't want to be in the same room with that idiot.

"Shar, mind if I borrow your car?" asked Martin. He stood at the kitchen sink, sweat beading up on his pitted face. Those acne scars made him look far older than he was.

"What are you doing?" Sharon noticed that he was running hot water over his arm.

"I'm trying to get this stupid cat tattoo off my arm. That kid Martha babysits for got this thing in a gumball machine. I can't get it to come off." Martin scrubbed furiously at the black smudge.

Sharon walked out of hearing range, into the bedroom. She didn't bother to answer when Martin asked again if he could borrow her car.

She peeled off her damp clothing and dug out her favorite flannel nightshirt. She slipped under the bed sheets, tucking the comforter under her chin. In a few short minutes she was deeply sleeping, snoring steadily.

31

~~~Digging Deeper~~~

Dan dreaded returning to the Virtual Memories building, but he was hopeful that Lamont would be busy with a client. He checked the schedule. Whew! Yes, Lamont would be booked for the rest of the evening.

Dan found Lamont's office door ajar. He quickly went in and shut the door behind him. He figured the sound of someone at the knob would give him enough time to shut off the computer.

Dan had disconnected his own office computer from the network, so he'd have a ready excuse to be in Lamont's office if anyone should come in before he had time to shut down. He hoped no one would.

Dan studied the crumbled note he'd crammed into his pocket from earlier in the day. Ten digits.

Maybe it's not an account number like he'd earlier thought.

It looks like another password.

He scrolled back to the 'enter password' command and typed in the ten digit number. Bingo! The computer started churning, calling up a file.

Dan groaned. It was the same file he'd already seen, Sharon's session.

No, wait.

He studied the screen in horror. No, this is a part he hadn't seen, the last segment of her session. He watched, mesmerized by the coldness of the woman before him. Ice must run through her veins.

Dan copied the new information onto a disk. Serena would want to see this. And then they would turn everything over to the police.

32

~~~Ready~~~

Serena dipped her fries into the container, enjoying the ritual. She smiled sweetly. "Dan is on his way here."

"Good." Karyn watched Serena's feasting. "What are you putting on your fries?"

"Mayonnaise."

"Mayonnaise? Oh no, Serena! You must be joking." Karyn scrunched up her face, imagining the total fat content of Serena's snack. She could almost *hear* the arteries clogging.

"Really. They do this in Europe."

"Eew. That's pretty gross." Karyn sipped her ice water. She heard Dan at the door and let him in.

"Well, I think we've got her. It's amazing."

Dan said as he walked toward Serena. "I know why she owed Lamont. He was covering for her."

"What are you talking about? Covering up for what?" Serena said, wiping her hands on the thighs of her jeans. She went through more jeans this way.

"Those numbers I found turned out to be a password. Lamont had saved the rest of her session with that password." Dan said breathlessly.

"Why would he hide the rest of her session? Did you find something strange in there?" Karyn asked.

"If any of our clients use their fantasy sessions to act out criminal behavior, our policy is to report that to the police." Dan said mysteriously.

"And she acted out something?" said Karyn.

"Yeah. That rule was in place, just in case. I guess Lamont wanted to protect her, must have taken a liking to her." Dan said, relishing in all the details of his sleuthing.

"So what did she act out?" Serena said impatiently.

Dan puffed his cheeks with air and let it out. "She killed her mother in law."

Karyn gasped.

"A greedy vipor." said Serena tonelessly.

"Yeah, that's it." Dan agreed.

"How?" Serena asked.

"Poison. She walked right into the hospital, gave Helen Miller some fancy candy. Sat right there and watched her eat it." Dan said.

"How do you know she poisoned the candy?" Serena said. "Is there proof?"

"The fantasy shows her doing it, before she

goes to the hospital. And after Helen eats the candy..." Dan looked down at his new brown loafers, new shoes to replace the ones that squeaked when he walked.

Serena gasped, eyes open wide. "The fantasy actually shows the woman dying?"

Dan shifted his weight uncomfortably. "Yes. The fantasy jumps forward, with a skip in the frame, to the, uh, end."

"What a sicko! Imagine Sharon creating a fantasy of this detail and watching it!" Karyn said.

"I'm disturbed by all of this." Serena said slowly.

"Well, me too!" Karyn agreed.

"No, I mean... Sharon told Bill that she didn't expect to owe Lamont much longer. I think it's possible that she has given up on trying to get Jack's share of the money, and is now in a hurry to get *whatever* share she can." Serena said.

"Oh *my*!" Karyn gasped.

Dan said, "What can we do to stop her?"

"It's time to get the police involved," said Serena.

"Well, we sure have enough to take to the police, right? I mean, we know the motive, we have those disks for evidence, and we even have a witness if Bill will testify." Karyn said.

"Oh he'll testify, he's a weasel. He wants immunity for his own part in this." Dan snorted.

"Yeah, we have everything we need, including the gun that Jack had. It was traced back to Vince." Serena said.

"Does Vince know anything?" Karyn asked.

"No, I don't think so. The police will check

him out, but I doubt he had any idea what she was up to." Serena said.

"Why did someone give Jack a gun?" Karyn said. "How does the gun come in to all of this?"

"I think Sharon was aware that her plan to mess with Jack's marriage failed, but that Jack was after Bill. Why not use Jack to get rid of Bill? She didn't need Bill any more." Serena cracked her knuckles, a habit that made her hands ache.

"I think you're right. And if Jack killed Bill, that could mess up Jack's marriage after all. Maybe she was trying to get at Jack that way." Dan said.

"What are we waiting for, who knows when Sharon will act," Karyn said anxiously. She rubbed her hands together.

"Let me call George first. I'd like him to hear what we have, to help Jack and Elizabeth's civil case against Virtual Memories, if they choose to go ahead with that." Serena said. She picked up the phone.

George was on his way out of the office when he got Serena's call. He picked it up on the first ring, "Yeah, George Bowmann."

"George, it's Serena. I have you on my speaker phone, with Karyn and Dan here."

"Yeah, your voice sounds far away, I hate speaker phones." George snatched up a ballpoint pen and started clicking it on top of the desk. *Click, click Click, click.*

"Whine, whine. Anyway, I have some interesting developments, that you might want to know about." Serena updated George on all the new discoveries.

"My, my, you've been a busy little detective, haven't you?" George teased.

"Nah, not too much. Karyn and Dan have done a lot of work on this case." Serena nodded toward Karyn and Dan, with a smile of appreciation for each.

"Actually, I've been meaning to call you. Jack has expressed to me that he would like to make a deal with Virtual. He's willing to make a quick settlement if they clean up their act, and put Dan in as their head guy there, whatever title that may be." George cleared his throat. "What'll you say, Dan?"

Dan leaned toward the speaker phone, startled by the news. "*Me?* Why me?"

"Jack likes you, likes Virtual Memories. Wants to see it get past this. Are you interested?"

Dan shrugged, "Yeah, I guess. If they go for it, I'll take the job."

"Good man. I've already begun initial discussion with Virtual, they seem open to the idea. They don't want a law suit."

"Well, thanks. I didn't expect this." Dan said. He grinned. Smilin' Dan would be wearing purple again.

"You can thank Jack. Also, Serena, take me off the speaker phone."

Serena did. "Yes?"

"I believe we had a bet."

"Yep."

"And you won." George cleared his throat.

"Sure did. It was no joke."

"It was no joke."

"Sure wasn't."

"OK, I'll take you out to dinner. Where do you want to go?"

"Hmm."

"Mexican? Italian? Greek?"

"How about Pizza Hut?"

"*Pizza Hut?* Really?"

"I like pizza."

"OK." George laughed, amused by this intriguing woman as always. "Pizza Hut it is."

"I gotta call Jack, let him in on everything we've found. We have enough to call the DA now."

"Be careful." George said gently.

"Why, George, you sound like you might care about me." Serena said smugly.

"Yeah, well, let the police take it from here." George said, clicking the pen.

"Of course." Serena smiled. *Gotcha!* she thought happily.

Serena's next call was to Jack. He too answered on the first ring, on his way out the door. "Hello?"

"Jack, this is Serena Wilcox. I need to talk to you about some new developments in your case." Serena used her professional cool tone.

Jack held the phone cord away from Kimmie, who was swinging the cord gleefully. "Serena, I'm on my way out to see Mom. The hospital called. She's not doing well and wants to see me."

Serena could hear the baby crying in the

background. Jack sounded stressed. "I'm sorry to hear that, Jack."

Serena paused respectfully, then added, "I do need to tell you that we are ready to present our findings to the district attorney's office. I'd like to go ahead and do that right away. It's rather urgent."

"OK, do what you need to do." Jack covered the phone with his hand. "Honey, you and the kids can go ahead and get in the car, I'll be there in a minute."

"I'll do that. Call me when you are ready to meet with me." Serena said gently. "And Jack? You take care, OK?"

33

~~~Sweet Justice~~~

Jack held his mother's hand. She looked so tired, so weary of the pain. "Jack, I want to talk to you about something."

"Yes?" Jack swallowed hard, fighting back tears that welled in his eyes. He didn't want to make things harder for his mother.

"I made some changes in my will."

"That's your right, Mom. I trust you to do what you think is best." Jack hated to talk about her will.

"I've decided to give my money to charity. Oh, I'll still give the grandchildren nice trust funds for their college education, but I'd hate to see my three children burdened with the pressure of too much money." Helen couldn't meet his eyes.

Jack was puzzled. "OK, Mom, whatever you want. You know that I don't care about the money."

She looked up at her son, relieved that he wasn't upset. "Yes, I know. You and Elizabeth are doing fine on your own. I had such a hard time in my marriage to your dad. All because of that money. My mother-in-law thought I married him for the money. It was never about the money, I married him for love."

"I know, Mom." Jack took her hand.

"I don't want you to have the pressure that having too much money brings. And I'd hate to see that spider Sharon get her hands on the money. As bad as she is to Vince, she'd be even worse with money." Helen closed her eyes.

"Mom, don't worry about any of this. I'm sure Sharon will get what's coming to her one of these days." Jack kissed his mother on the forehead and pressed her frail hand close to his chest.

~~~ ~~~

Sharon was arrested in the parking lot of the hospital that very same day with an unopened box of beautifully gift-wrapped chocolates. The chocolates later tested positive for poison.

Sharon learned about Helen's death, a peaceful passing in the night, from her cell as she awaited trial. She couldn't say that she was sorry for her death. She only wished that she had helped it along. She waited anxiously for Vince to visit with news about the will.

But Vince never came. He sent her divorce papers, and a note:

Mom changed her will. She gave the kids a trust fund, but the bulk of her estate has been earmarked for charitable organizations.

A hideous shriek escaped from Sharon's evil lips. It took three guards to hold her down while she flailed her arms and kicked her pretty feet. They dragged her off in a straight jacket. Under heavy sedation, Sharon spent her days in a psychiatric hospital for the criminally insane, dreaming of the money she would never have.

Gene Play

An excerpt from book one of the Serena Wilcox Mysteries

"I said, where is my husband!" shrieked Rita.

"You mean your ex-husband?" Karyn held the phone about an inch away from her ear. Rita's nasal voice was annoying enough when heard at a normal conversational level, when she was upset her voice was shrill and nasty.

There was a momentary silence in which both women held out for the other to be the first one to speak.

Karyn sighed. "So what do you want, Rita?"

"I need to speak to Richard immediately and you can tell him that I'm getting sick of his crap."

"He's not here, if that's what you want to know."

"Well then I bet I know just where he is." The resounding click that followed freed Karyn from further conversation with this woman. What had Rick ever seen in her? It was obvious that Rita was a pathetic woman who would never be happy unless everyone else was miserable.

Karyn decided to take a midday bubble bath. Immersing herself in warm water scented with lilac bath beads was the perfect way to undo the effects of a bout with Rita. She rubbed a pink bar of Camay soap over her legs until a
satisfying lather developed. Then she began to shave her legs with a mint green disposable razor in neat even lines.

"Aargh!" Blood dribbled down Karyn's right leg. "I haven't done that in years. Where are the Band-Aids?" she said in the monotone murmur that she used when she was alone and talking to herself.

Karyn stepped out of the tub, making a wet soapy mess on the floor that she knew she would hear about later from Rick.

"I know I've got Band-Aids somewhere... I could have sworn they were right back here." Karyn stretched her five-foot-one frame to reach the large wooden medicine cabinet that was mounted over a designer jade toilet bowl. She tossed aside a tube of BenGay and several near-empty bottles of pain reliever. Groping around on the top shelf that she couldn't quite reach, her hand hit something that was stuck to the back of the medicine cabinet.

"What in the world..." she muttered. She felt a thick wad of what she could only assume was duct tape. "This thing is taped on. What is this?"

Karyn wrapped a towel around her and grabbed some toilet tissue for the nick on her leg. Then she hobbled into the kitchen, keeping the towel from slipping with one hand and opening cabinet drawers with the other until she found a pair of scissors. Perched on the back of the toilet, she squatted in a crazy stance to bring the medicine cabinet close to eye-level. She opened the scissors as wide as they would part and scraped away at the duct tape that held the tiny package to the back of the medicine cabinet.

The package was about the size of Karyn's hand. It looked like a manila folder that had been folded over several times. It was wedged behind one of the shelves in the cabinet.

She wasn't making any progress with the scissors so she grabbed a pair of heavy duty toe clippers and jabbed at the tape. Just when Karyn had resigned herself to removing the shelf to get it out, the package flew from her hand and landed with a splunk into the tub of lilac-scented water.

Camp Conviction

It was the perfect family vacation, a religious retreat.

Husbands and wives came home ready to make changes in their lives.
No more TV in their homes.
No more rock music.
No more public schooling for their children.

And a sudden interest in protesting the sale of a few acres of land.

Look for Camp Conviction, the next Serena Wilcox mystery. Updates about the Serena Wilcox Mysteries are posted to Natalie Buske Thomas' author site at: http://aol/members/writernbt.html

NORMANDALE COMMUNITY COLLEGE
LIBRARY
9700 FRANCE AVENUE SOUTH
BLOOMINGTON, MN 55431-4399